PENGUIN BOOKS

MRS HARTLEY AND
THE GROWTH CENTRE

Philippa Gregory holds a doctorate from the University of Edinburgh for her research into eighteenth-century literature. She trained as a journalist and worked for the BBC. She lives with her family in West Sussex. Philippa Gregory is best known for her eighteenth-century novels, *Wideacre*, *The Favoured Child* and *Meridon*, which together make up the bestselling saga of the Lacey family and are published by Penguin. *The Wise Woman*, her new historical novel set in the Tudor period, is published by Viking and forthcoming in Penguin. She has also written several children's books, *Princess Florizella* (Puffin 1989), *Florizella and the Wolves*, and *Florizella and the Giant*.

D0892337

MRS HARTLEY AND
THE GROWTH CENTRE

PHILIPPA GREGORY

PENGUIN BOOKS

PENGUIN BOOKS

Published by the Penguin Group
27 Wrights Lane, London w8 5tz, England
Penguin Books USA Inc., 375 Hudson Street, New York, New York 10014, USA
Penguin Books Australia Ltd, Ringwood, Victoria, Australia
Penguin Books Canada Ltd, 10 Alcorn Avenue, Toronto, Ontario, Canada m4v 3b2
Penguin Books (NZ) Ltd, 182–190 Wairau Road, Auckland 10, New Zealand

Penguin Books Ltd, Registered Offices: Harmondsworth, Middlesex, England

Published in Penguin Books 1992
1 3 5 7 9 10 8 6 4 2

Printed in England by Clays Ltd, St Ives plc
Filmset in 10/13 pt Monophoto Plantin

WEDNESDAY NIGHT

Professor Charles Hartley leaned back in his chair and watched his wife progress through the languid motions of the Dance of the Seven Veils. In the background, from the Hartleys' tasteful black ash hi-fi system came the whine of an Eastern flute, like a dog shut on the wrong side of a door. Alice Hartley revolved slowly, her large black-ringed eyes expectantly on her husband, her broad feet treading the carpet. Charles Hartley stifled a yawn.

He was not aroused. Deep in the recesses of his baggy boxer shorts The Phallus – the proud symbol of the Professor's innate superiority over half of the population of the world – lay quiescent, a dozing puppy. There was no urgency. There was no hurry. Mrs Alice Hartley wore several layers of diaphanous petticoats and gauzes beneath her flowing kaftan, and tonight, as a special treat for Charles's forty-fourth birthday, she had added several scarves trimmed with beads and bells around her neck, waist, and wrists, a djellaba over her head, and a collegiate scarf tied purdah-wise across the lower part of her face.

She would be hours getting that lot off, Professor Hartley thought sourly, and settled himself deeper into his padded rocker-chair. Hours and hours, he thought gloomily and his imagination strayed – as it so often did – to little Miranda Bloomfeather who could step out of her t-shirt and tight blue jeans in fifteen seconds flat – and often, deliciously, did.

Professor Hartley was at that time in his life when a man demands of himself what is the meaning of life, asking: 'For what was I born? And is this all there is? And what of the great quests which have motivated men through the ages? Where am I going? And what is the Nature of Individualism? Or, more simply: Who am I?'

Like all men who courageously confront great questions of identity and truth, Professor Hartley came to one conclusion. Unerringly, untiringly he struggled through his boredom and his despair until he found the source of his discontent, the spring of his angst, his own private darkness. It was all the fault of his wife.

Alice, he sincerely felt, was part of his past. Part of his struggling, underfunded, undergraduate past. While Miranda, with her pert little bum and skimpy clothes, was undoubtedly The Future. Certainly the disturbing and erotic dreams which awoke him nightly with The Phallus making a little tent of the continental quilt were deeply symbolic, meaning – he was sure – that it was time for a shift of perspective. Time for growth, time for rediscovery, time to change. In other words (in the crude simplicities of lay-person's speech): Professor Hartley was tired of Alice; and wanted Miranda instead.

He planned to explore with Alice, in a free and open adult discussion, exactly where their relationship was failing, and what were his underlying needs. Indeed, he had mentally reserved their next counselling session for just such a revelation. He planned casually to steer the session towards a discussion about growth and change and then lure Alice into expressing a readiness to try a new form of marriage – a more open relationship. Then he planned to confront her with her just-stated wish to leave him; and nobly offer her a divorce. By the time Alice had sorted out what he was doing and what were his intentions Professor Hartley reckoned to have packed her things and changed the locks.

Not that he ever acknowledged – even in his quietest moments – the simple truth that he was deserting Alice. Professor Hartley was educated and nourished in a world which, on the whole, took the male viewpoint as the norm and the female view (when it is offered which, God knows, is rare enough) as aberrant. His boredom with Alice and his lust for Miranda he perceived fondly, as the Spirit of the Age, and therefore inevitable. He told himself that Alice too was ready for change. She was ready to go away, he fondly reassured himself. She was always trailing off for study weekends with the Well Women's Group, with the Open University, for her training as a New Age counsellor, for her vegan retreats.

3

Professor Charles Hartley nodded judiciously. At the deep emotional levels where, as a Professor of Psychology, he alone was expert, he knew that Alice had already abandoned him. What he was doing was characteristic male behaviour: hunting down the truth about their lives. He was exhibiting the male courage which makes men leaders, explorers, kings. He was the heir to huntsmen, cavemen, and particularly entrepreneurial monkeys. He had the courage to confront this issue instead of concealing it – as Alice wished to conceal it – behind the now empty rituals of living together.

Alice used the typical, cowardly, female tactic of behaving as if their relationship was thriving, behaving as if she still cared for him, devoting her life to him as usual. Professor Hartley recognized her day-to-day care of him, her support of his work, and her unfailing, indeed excessive readiness to make love as the despicable ploy it was. It was Alice's innate female cowardice that made her love him and support him and protect him from the outside world. It was her failure of vision. It would be healthy for them both to break this routine and bourgeois life. Charles stretched longingly and The Phallus lifted its head like a dog when his master calls 'walkies!'

When Alice was gone . . . Miranda could move in.

Charles thanked God (a Being remarkably resembling Charles Hartley in appearance, logic, and priorities) that he was not a promiscuous man. Charles knew from his studies in sociology and anthropology that he was a serial monogamist. Charles thought that men who had sexual relations with many women lacked control and self-discipline. He knew that the natural way, the proper way, especially for a natural leader of other men, is one woman at a time – the duration of that time depending of course on the desirability of the woman and the availability of alternatives. This, Charles knew, is not promiscuity. It is not even sexual liberalism. It is Natural Selection, and right now Natural Selection and the whole Darwinian structure of the Laws of Evolution were supporting Charles's decision to dump Alice and replace her with Miranda.

He smiled at the thought, and Alice, mistaking his expression for arousal, came a little closer and danced within reach of his slack fingers. She took three steps to the right and pointed one large white foot, she took three steps to the left and widened her dark kohl-rimmed eyes, she came even closer and, provocatively, winsomely, trailed one of her gauze scarves across his face. The little beaten coins of gold at the fringe tapped unpleasantly on his cheek and then one struck him, painfully, in the right eye.

'For God's sake, Alice!' he exploded irritably. 'Do you have to?'

Alice shuddered to a sudden halt, open-mouthed. 'What?' she demanded as if she could not believe her ears.

Charles looked at her. She was a dark-haired, large-eyed, full-bodied woman, exotic in her ethnic

5

prints and gipsy shawls. Her cheeks were rosy with exercise and her kohl-rimmed eyes were wide with astonishment.

'What?' she said again.

'I am sick of you,' Charles said simply, throwing strategy to the winds and telling the truth for once. 'I am sick of the awful stews you make, and your herbal remedies. I am sick of tea made from flowers, and carrot cake which sticks to the roof of my mouth for hours, even days, after I have finished eating. I am sick of sleeping with the curtains open so that you can have moonlight on your face and be in touch with your lunar cycle. I am sick of your trailing dresses and your weird coloured pop-socks. I want a divorce.'

Alice stood as still as if she had been turned into a pillar of genuine, unrefined rock salt. She pulled the stripy college scarf away from her mouth and, to his horror, Charles saw she was smiling. Worse than that – oh God, much worse – she was laughing at him.

'Miranda Bloomfeather,' she said with uncanny prescience.

'I don't know what you mean,' Charles said weakly. He tried, without success, to erase the picture of Miranda Bloomfeather's brown buttocks from his mind. Despite his professorial chair in Applied Psychology he could not rid himself of a superstitious belief that his wife could read his thoughts.

'Miranda Bloomfeather,' Alice said again. 'A

natural D. You gave her A minus last term. You must think we are all as half-witted as she is.'

A vision of Miranda Bloomfeather's silky tanned thighs pressed demurely side-by-side under her denim miniskirt dashed through Charles's mind like a wasp through a picnic. He resolutely turned his eyes and thoughts to the pile of the carpet under his wife's bare splayed feet. He did not know whom she meant by 'we' and he feared she had been indulging in vulgar gossip with Miranda Bloomfeather's personal tutor – a fellow-member of his wife's homeopathic consciousness-raising group. Another nut-case woman, he thought miserably.

He tried to recapture the initiative by a swift return to the discussion he had planned. 'We have both changed, Alice,' he said sonorously. 'We have both grown during the time of our marriage. Indeed, we have grown *because* of our marriage. Now we both have new needs. You and I together must think how we are going to satisfy these needs – yours as well as mine.'

'Miranda Bloomfeather,' Alice said, smiling broadly. She opened her scarlet mouth showing large white teeth. 'Ha. Ha. Ha.'

'Now look here,' said Charles. 'I am trying to have a serious and civilized conversation with you, Alice. It is nothing to do with Miranda. That is a quite separate issue which I will discuss when you are feeling calmer.'

As usual, the suggestion that Alice was not calm sent her into a towering and uncontrollable rage.

'Calm?' she shrieked. 'I am calm! But I'll tell you what I'm not! I'm not clammy! I'm not creepy! I'm not an impotent old stick who can only get it up with a nineteen-year-old on his office floor!'

Charles could feel a throbbing in his temples which meant that Alice was giving him one of his tension headaches. 'We won't talk now.' He got up swiftly from his chair and went towards the door. 'I'm going to bed,' he said. 'I can feel a headache coming on. I deplore your tone and language, Alice. I shall be raising this at our marital counselling session tomorrow.'

'Who started it?' she demanded instantly. 'Who started up about the carrot cake? Who wanted a divorce five seconds ago, and now wants a quiet life?'

Charles turned, his hand on the door. 'I do,' he said. He meant he wanted the divorce but Alice screeched with laughter at his assent.

'I'll give you a quiet life!' she exclaimed. With one bracelet-manacled hand she swept the blue Ionian pottery vases off the mantelpiece so they crashed into the fireplace. The bunch of very old dried flowers in the cold grate exploded into dust and sterile pollen.

'There!' she shouted defiantly.

Charles looked at her with weary satisfaction. 'You just *make* work for yourself, Alice,' he said and went out, closing the door behind him with the restrained click of a man who knows himself to be in the right.

'Ha!' Alice said to the unresponsive door. Less certainly, with a little quaver in her voice she said it again: 'Ha!'

She could hear him going softly upstairs, his suede shoes making little crunching noises on the cork matting. Ten years ago he would have wrestled her down to the floor and taken her with passion and anger on the hearthrug among the shards of china and the dried flowers. Five years ago he would have walked out, but she would have run after him in tears and they would have made up in the comfort of their large pine bed. Even at their most recent quarrel, last month, he had pompously departed but then thought of something so irresistible that he had come back in to say: 'And another thing . . .' and they had fought on until they reached a compromise which each could privately call victory.

Now she stood still while the dust settled and the Arabic music moaned on. He did not come back; not even with some cutting phrase assembled on the stairs and too good to leave unsaid.

And she let him go.

Liar that he was, Charles was right for once, she thought moodily, stirring her big toe among the shreds of long-dead hydrangea. They had changed. Perhaps it was time to move on.

But she was damned if he was going to have it all his own way! Alice was not one of those injured wives who wear betrayal like a mourning brooch. She could not face the thought of Charles's

9

colleagues' muted condolences when she met them in the university health food shop. They would rally round to let her weep on their shoulders while they patted her back and rubbed discreetly against her front. They would sympathize to her face, and when their wives were listening; but when they were alone with Charles they would say 'ho, ho, ho'.

'Ho, ho, ho,' Alice whispered resentfully into the quiet room. 'Ho bloody ho.'

It was so *ageing* to be left for a nineteen-year-old, she thought miserably. She looked at herself in the mirror over the marble mantelpiece. The lights were darkened and the reflection was kind. But no one could look from Alice to Miranda Bloomfeather and have the least doubt that Charles Hartley had swopped his old wife for a young mistress. Alice rested her face against the cold surface of the mantelpiece and struggled against the profound blow to her deepest self – her vanity.

There was a tap on the front door. It was so soft that for a moment she thought she had misheard it. But then it came again, louder, two taps. Alice glanced at her reflection in the mirror, impatiently tweaked off the djellaba, threw back the mass of her dark hair and went out into the hall and opened the door.

There was a young man on the doorstep. When Alice opened the door he pulled off his woolly bobble-hat and smiled nervously.

'Oh!' he said. His voice was light, shy. His smile was engaging. His close-cropped brown hair was curly, his pebble glasses magnified his eyes, which were pale and blue. Alice felt a rush of unexpected and uncontrollable lust.

'Mrs Hartley!' he exclaimed. 'I am sorry to trouble you so late, but we were moving scenery later than we meant.'

Alice noted the large removal van behind him. She tossed back her hair and glowed at him. 'That's quite all right,' she said. 'Won't you come in? I don't quite know what this is all about?'

He stepped lightly over the doorstep. The hall was narrow. Alice turned so that her large rounded breasts brushed against his denim jacket.

'It's Suffix Theatre Players,' he said. His voice quavered into a little squeak but he soon had it under control again. 'We're doing a play "The Intruder", and we need a psychiatrist's couch. Your husband very kindly said we could borrow his. I've come to collect it. But perhaps I'm a bit late.'

Alice gave a little gasp. 'Wait here,' she ordered and she spun on her bare heel and pattered quickly upstairs. A faint tinkling sound from the little bells and the coins followed her as she opened the door to the spare bedroom at the front of the house where she guessed Charles had retreated.

He was lying flat on his back in the spare bed. A small brown bottle of Mogadon pills beside his bed indicated that he had avoided a further confrontation with Alice by hiding in deep sleep. The slow sensual grunts which came from his half-parted lips indicated to a wife who knew him well that he was not hiding from Miranda Bloomfeather.

Alice's dark gaze hardened. Then she closed the door softly and went back downstairs. The moon face of the young student looked up at her as she came down like some dark goddess descending from an inner place of sacrifice.

'Professor Hartley's asleep,' she said sweetly. 'But I'll help you with the couch. I'll just slip some sandals on.'

The student dumbly nodded.

'What's your name?' Alice asked. She pulled up the layers of kaftan and silk petticoats to tie the straps of her sandals. The student caught a glimpse of pale knee, of pale thigh, of darker – could it be? surely not? –

'M-M-M-Michael Coulter,' he said.

Alice stroked down her layers of skirts. 'Michael,' she said, as if the word had some hidden meaning. 'How lovely! My name is Alice.'

'He – llo,' Michael said weakly. He had a terrible feeling that he was behaving like a wimp.

'Now,' Alice said determinedly. 'Do you have much space in that lovely big van of yours?'

Michael gulped and waved his arms vaguely in the air to indicate wide open spaces. The van was quite empty. He had hired it in error, thinking he was getting a little tailgate wagon. When he had come to collect it he had found a vehicle the size of a pantechnicon and a bill to match.

'Would you do me a favour?' Alice breathed.

Michael goggled, nodded.

'I'm moving house,' Alice said. 'Could you help

me take a few, just a few of my special things now? I'll come back for the rest in the morning. I'll help you with the couch – and would the Professor's desk be of any use? – and then we can put some of my little things in.'

Alice rolled up her skirt at the waistband. Michael took off his jacket. They set to work.

They started with the study. Alice insisted that the Suffix Theatre Players should have anything which would add authenticity to their set. They stripped the study of all the furniture, the rugs, and even the Professor's framed degrees off the wall and the curtains from the window.

'Charles won't mind!' Alice said blithely.

They moved on to the dining-room, the kitchen, and the sitting-room. They had to leave the piano: it was a baby grand.

'It seems a shame,' Alice said sorrowfully. 'It looks so lonely there, all on its own, with no other furniture in the room and the carpet up off the floor.'

'Come back for it tomorrow,' Michael gasped. There was a sheen of cold sweat on his pale face from the effort of humping his end of the Wilton carpet. Alice was flushed, nothing more.

'Upstairs,' she said. She put a hand on Michael's bare forearm. 'Very, very quietly,' she cautioned him. 'We don't want to wake the Professor. This is going to be a lovely surprise for him in the morning.' She gleamed in the half-light of the hall, thinking of Charles waking to a house stripped bare of all the carefully accumulated possessions of a lifetime. 'He's going to think the fairies have been!' she said gaily.

Michael, hypnotized and hyperventilating from effort, nodded dumbly.

Alice led the way. The door to the spare bedroom was tight shut. Behind it, locked in dreams, Charles bore Miranda Bloomfeather to the ground on the white shores of a tropical beach. The towering waves broke over them, Miranda shuddered in grateful ecstasy. The crash when Michael dropped his end of the double pine bed frame was the Pacific rollers beating on the coral seashore. Alice's squeak of alarm when she lost her grip on her end of the wardrobe was Miranda crying like one of the gulls on 'Desert Island Discs', 'Again! Again! Charles, again!'

Michael and Alice stood on the doorstep. The house gutted and dark stood empty behind them.

'Could you give me a lift?' Alice asked.

Michael's body was shaking like unset jelly from the strain of unaccustomed exertion. 'Of course, Mrs Hartley,' he said gallantly. 'I'd love to.'

'I'll get my cape,' Alice said and went back into the house. Michael collapsed into his seat in the cab. He started the van to get the heater going, he rested his head in his hands on the steering-wheel. He let out a soft sob of fatigue. He had never worked so hard in all his life. He could not have believed he was capable of such hard work. But Mrs Hartley was a wonder! And at her age, and everything!

Inside the house Alice took her cape from the hook under the stairs. It was the only garment left. All Charles's clothes, like all Charles's books, pictures, notes, sporting trophies, horse brasses, like all Charles's furniture and curtains, were packed up and loaded in the providential van. Alice stole around the house with her cape wrapped close against the chill, confirming that everything, yes, everything, was safely packed up. Only one room of the house was untouched. The spare bedroom where Charles snuffled and dreamed of a tropical paradise and Miranda.

It seemed such a shame to leave the job half-done. Alice hesitated outside the door once more. She opened it softly and peeped in. Charles stirred in his sleep and turned his face towards the door. Alice crept in. She stood in silence and waited in case he should sense her presence. Waited for one word from him, one word of reconciliation, one word of tenderness.

'Miranda!' Charles said through clogged lips.

It was enough! It would have been enough for any woman of spirit. Alice slid over to the window and raised the lower half. She tumbled Charles's clothes out into the darkened garden. The book by his bedside, the bedside reading lamp. She was sorry that the bedside table was too big, but the rug beneath the bed rolled up and tumbled out easily. Each one of the drawers from the chest of drawers fitted lengthwise as if they had been specifically designed to fling from windows into the silent night.

Charles in the bed was far away. Michael in the van was dozing with weariness, waking only once to gaze upwards, bemused, as a bedside lamp and three drawers fell lightly through the moonlight to smash into the flowerbeds of the front garden. Only Alice, with a peaceful, satisfied smile on her face, knew that the spare bedroom was as derelict and bare as the rest of the house which Charles had once called home.

She crept downstairs again and closed the front door softly behind her, then she hitched up her flowing skirts and climbed into the driver's cab beside Michael.

He came to with a start. 'Where can I take you, Mrs Hartley?' he asked.

Alice lay back and closed her eyes. 'Let's go to your place,' she said silkily. 'I want to know you, Michael. I want to plunge into your deepest essences.'

Michael was not precisely a virgin. He had, for instance, been to bed with three girls. One in the third term of his first year when the combination of hot sun and unexpectedly potent lager had numbed Michael's nerves and her resistance; one in the first term of his second year after the excitement of a dress rehearsal of *Measure for Measure*; and one in the second term because she was new to the Theatre Players and mistook him for someone important. On each occasion Michael had suffered from that common scourge of young Englishmen which is caused by insufficient action and excessive imagination. The ladies, of course, had suffered also.

Weeks, indeed months of celibacy had not quietened Michael's over-active libido and from the moment he had seen Mrs Hartley's white knee, white thigh and dark (but surely it couldn't have been?) he had been in a state of sexual arousal so extreme that he had found the strength to hold his end of the wardrobe when Alice had dropped hers. When he learned he was to take her and the furniture to some unknown destination he was in a fever of lust. Not that he desired to do anything with, or to, Alice Hartley.

Oh no.

Michael was desperate to get back to his own bed to enjoy the thought of that white knee, white thigh and darker, darker, darker – perhaps it really was!

But when Alice leaned back and shut her eyes and asked to go to his place, Michael lost all desire and nearly fainted with fear.

His bedsitting-room was in a purpose-built student hall of residence not far from the stripped shell which had once been the Hartleys' house. Michael drove with manic concentration, partly because he was afraid of the height and weight of the vehicle and the way Professor Hartley's furniture shifted when they went around corners; but also because driving helped him to keep his imagination from the question of what Mrs Hartley meant by wanting to plunge into his deepest essences. At her age, she surely couldn't mean . . . but perhaps she did?

Michael eased the van to a standstill and switched off the engine. The big vehicle shuddered. Alice lifted her head and opened her dark eyes.

'Take me,' she said.

Michael wound down the window, furiously rotating the handle in error for the door handle. Alice smiled mysteriously, the smile of a woman who is flowing with deeper forces than any mere man could comprehend. She opened the door her side and dropped down to the ground. After a moment's thought she reached inside the cab and pulled out the djellaba and college scarf so despised by the abandoned Professor. Wrapping the djellaba around her head and the scarf around her mouth she followed Michael up the echoing well of stairs, down the fluorescent-lit corridors to the doorway to his room, and inside.

'It's not much,' Michael started nervously, indicating the cramped single bed and the small desk. On the narrow window-sill stood a lone carton of date-expired milk and a solitary pot of decaying yoghurt.

'Do you have music?' Alice asked. Her voice was slurred, deeper. She seemed taller.

Michael gave a little whimper of apprehension and fell back on the bed, pressing, as he did, the play button on his little cassette player. The tinny sound of folk music filled the silent room and once again, for the second time that evening, Alice rotated slowly in the sensuous steps of the Dance of the Seven Veils.

But what a change in the attention of the audience!

Michael was transfixed, his mouth wide open, the round lenses of his glasses misting up as his little panting breaths condensed on the glass. Alice, casting a languorous sideways glance over her shoulder, saw the colour drain from his face, and then saw him flush pink as a rose as she tossed aside another multicoloured scarf to lie in a heap in the corner.

Michael gulped. Nothing like this had ever happened in his life before. He had never even *heard* of anything like this ever happening to anyone before. He had never even read about it in books ever.

He did not know it was the Dance of the Seven Veils – if pressed for a name he would have thought it was the Dance of the One Hundred and Forty-Two Veils, as Alice Hartley spun around faster and faster, and scarves flew from her as if torn away by centrifugal force, until she was dancing in the centre of his room surrounded by a hailstorm of rainbow silks, wearing nothing but her kaftan which she slowly undid at the neck and let drop and drop and drop over her grand white shoulders, her jogging warm breasts, her rounded belly, her proud broad hips, and her dark ... her dark ... her dark – it really was!

Michael Coulter pitched head first into his pillow and let out a despairing wail: 'Oh God! Too soon again!'

A younger woman (or one with somewhere else to go) might have flounced from the room; but Alice did not flounce.

A woman with higher expectations would have

been angry; but Alice had been married for years and was inured to sexual disappointment.

She excavated Michael's tearful face from his pillow, she stripped him, as efficient as an old-fashioned ward sister before the NHS reforms. She laid him on his back, spread-eagled and spent, and then with two skilled hands she plunged up to her elbows into his essences.

Alice Hartley had a small peculiarity – which Michael, despite his dazed and delirious state, could not help noticing. She seemed to have some especial use for his essences; for just when he arrived once more at crisis point, she arranged matters in such a way that The Phallus (which Michael knew famili-arly as 'Blinkie') was between her encouraging hands, and then she retreated to the corner where his little basin stood, her hands cupped before her as if she were transferring a rare and precious tropi-cal fish from one tank to another. Then Michael heard the noise of her briskly slapping cream into her face and neck.

Michael was a third-year student in the English Literature department – naturally his reading was superficial and scanty. He had no idea that semen is said to be a remarkably efficacious anti-wrinkle cream. He had no idea that one reason for Alice's loudly expressed delight was that she thought she had found an inexhaustible supply.

THURSDAY MORNING

They did not sleep well. The bed was too small for two to rest in comfort, especially when one of the pair was a statuesque and beautiful woman long neglected, and the other was a shrimpy and sexually-frustrated youth. By the time that Michael's window had lightened with the early sunlight of summer they were mutually satisfied, and mutually exhausted. They both believed themselves to be deeply in love.

There was an abrupt loud knocking on the door. Michael clutched at Alice wide-eyed.

'Could that be your husband, Mrs Hartley?' he asked in a frightened whisper.

Alice beamed with satisfaction at the thought. 'I don't know,' she said. 'You answer it, I'll hide by the sink.'

The sink in Michael's room was recessed in the wall. If Alice stood very still and breathed in and did not breathe out, she could not be seen in a casual inspection of the room from the door.

Michael nodded, bundled as many of the scarves

as he could grab under the bed, and opened the door.

'Urgent message,' said the porter. 'You Michael Coulter?'

'Yes,' said Michael.

'Urgent message from the Dean's secretary,' said the porter. 'Thought I'd bring it straight over.'

'Thank you,' Michael said. He took the envelope and came back into the room, closing the door behind him.

Alice was red-cheeked and gasping.

Michael turned the envelope over and over in his hands.

'I suppose I'd better open it,' he said.

She took it from him with a quick authoritative movement and passed her broad hand first one side of the envelope, and then the other.

'There is nothing in here which will distress you,' she said certainly. 'Objects have auras just as people do. There is nothing in here which will cause you any pain. This has a healthy aura. It will be news of a development for you, for growth. Nothing bad.'

Michael was deeply impressed. He opened the envelope with new confidence. It read:

REGRET TO INFORM YOU,
AUNTY SARAH NEAR DEATH.
COME AT ONCE.

It was signed 'Simmonds' with the letters 'GP' afterwards.

Michael looked blankly at Alice.

'Were you very close to your Aunty Sarah?' she asked.

Michael shook his head. 'I hardly know her,' he said. 'She is much older than my father, a funny old biddy who lives out in the old vicarage at Rithering. I've only been over once since I've been here. I should have gone more often I suppose.'

'There you are then!' Alice said triumphantly. 'The auras are never wrong. I said it was a healthy aura.'

'Not very healthy for Aunty Sarah,' Michael said reflectively.

Alice paused. 'She is just moving to another plane,' she said. 'Will you go and see her at once?'

'Will you come?' Michael asked quickly and then blushed. 'I mean', he said, 'I suppose you've got loads of other things to do, moving house and all that.'

Alice looked surprised, she had forgotten the furniture. She had, in any case, nowhere to go.

'That can wait,' she said. 'We do not yet know each other well, Michael, but I can promise you that I would never waste my time on trivial housewife details.' She hissed the word housewife through clenched teeth. She had not forgotten Charles's slight on her carrot cakes. 'Not when there are elemental forces at work. The great chasms of death and birth are around us all the time. We must be ready for them. I will come with you.'

Michael threw his arms around her naked waist and pressed his face into her neck. He felt a sudden stirring as if his deepest essences were ready for plunging again, but Alice gently disengaged herself.

'Not now,' she said softly. 'We must go to your Aunt. The old lady will be waiting for you, she may want your help to move her into a fresh astral plane. You must centre yourself, root yourself in the earthly elements. I will help you.'

Michael nodded obediently, put both feet into one trouser leg and fell to the floor.

Alice regarded him with affection. 'Get dressed,' she said. 'I have to go to the health centre and see someone. I'll be back in a few minutes.'

She threw her gown over her head and tied half a dozen scarves about her person, three on her head, one on each wrist, one at her waist, and slipped from the room.

Outside, the campus was quiet with the early-morning stillness of centres of great learning. Students were not yet awake and those faculty members who had survived the most recent wave of redundancies and were still clinging to salaries and offices were writing their novels, their guides to Provence, and malicious letters to specialist journals. Alice glided easily across the dew-soaked grass with her wide dancing stride and ran lightly up the steps to the university medical centre and into the counselling room.

Professor Hartley was at the window, he had been watching her. Sitting in his shadow was a small elderly woman in grey. She wore pale grey shoes, stone-grey tights under a buff-grey skirt.

Her shirt was grey silk, her cardigan was shapeless-grey. Her hair was natural grey. Her smile was professionally serene.

'Welcome, Alice,' she said kindly.

Alice tossed her an angry look. Her husband she totally ignored.

There was a short silence. Professor Hartley seethed in silence like a small culture of poisonous yeast.

'Shall I start?' the counsellor asked.

Alice, who had been gazing sulkily at her red varnished toes peeping through her golden sandals, glanced up and shrugged her broad shoulders. The Professor nodded.

'I notice you have arrived separately this morning,' the counsellor said, her voice carefully neutral. 'Would you tell me, Alice, why that is?'

Alice glowered at her. 'I imagine you know perfectly well.'

The counsellor's raised eyebrows and innocent look expressed total bafflement. 'What do you mean, Alice?' she asked with playgroup patience. 'Remember our rule here: no ambiguous statements!'

Alice jerked her head at Professor Hartley who was standing with his back to the window, blocking the light. 'I imagine Charles has told you that I have left him!' Alice said defiantly.

The counsellor put her head on one side like a small grey canary. 'And if he *had* told me, and please notice, Alice, that I do not say he *has* told me, what do you imagine that Charles would say about you?' she asked.

Alice laughed shortly. 'Oh no,' she said. 'Not again. I have wasted years trying to work out what Charles thinks. I have wasted a lifetime trying to please him.' She pointed an accusing finger at the counsellor. '*You* have wasted hours and hours trying to work out what Charles wants. I am here today to say only one thing: that I am not coming into this dreary room to have you two ganging-up on me any more.'

Charles Hartley pushed himself up off the window-sill, pulled a chair towards him, and sat down leaning forward earnestly, his hands clasped, as if he were praying for Alice's redemption. 'I don't know why you are so angry with Mrs Bland, Alice,' he said, in his special marital-counselling voice. 'It makes me wonder what it is that you are so angry about in yourself?'

'Oh no,' Alice said again. 'Not that one. I am *not* angry with myself. I am angry with you, Charles. You are pompous, you are a liar, and I will *not* be ditched by you for some stupid undergraduate.' Alice swung around on Mrs Bland. 'And you,' she said. 'You are One of Them!'

The counsellor's placid smile did not waver. Her eyes flicked to Professor Hartley as if seeking expert opinion. He nodded at her. 'Delusional Paranoia,' he said softly.

The counsellor's face grew yet more serene. 'Why are you abusing your husband, Alice?' she asked. She gave a little humble smile. 'And why are you insulting me?'

Alice choked on her anger. 'I don't trust either of you!' she said, stammering. 'You know! You both know! You both know what I am angry about!'

'And what is that?' asked Mrs Bland. She looked to Charles. His face was a portrait of hurt bafflement.

'What do we both know?' he asked gently.

'You both know that Charles is having sex with Miranda Bloomfeather. You both know that he wants a divorce. You both know that I left him last night. And you both should know that I am never, *never* going back!' Alice proclaimed.

Mrs Bland put in a wonderful performance of utter mystification. 'I think you had better explain this to me, Alice,' she said. 'I can assure you I know nothing of this!'

Alice hammered the arms of her chair with her fists. 'You do! You do!' she said, her voice rising with her frustration. 'I don't believe that Charles hasn't told you. Half the university knows about him and Miranda. Even *I* know!'

'Oh, I see now what is happening here,' Mrs Bland said gently. Alice glanced at her, momentarily hopeful.

'You have forgotten our little rule,' she said, smiling and holding up one finger. 'D'you remember which one I mean?'

Alice shook her head.

'Do you know which one I mean, Professor Hartley?' Mrs Bland asked him, smiling.

Charles smiled back, like a big child in a nursery

class who is prepared to play nicely to help the little ones learn. 'Would it be the one about not bringing gossip into our counselling sessions?' he asked.

Mrs Bland clasped her hands together as if struggling not to applaud. 'That's the one!' she said gaily. 'And anything which needs to be said, is to be said here and now.'

She turned to Alice. 'Now,' she said. 'Do you want to ask Professor Hartley about his relationship with his students?'

Alice was twisting a dark lock of hair around her finger, her face black. 'Yes,' she said sulkily.

Mrs Bland nodded. 'Go on then, Alice,' she said. 'Ask the Professor whatever it is you wish.'

Alice tugged on the lock of hair, and then looked directly at Charles. He leaned towards her, his face a picture of kindly concern.

'Do you want to divorce me?' she asked. 'Are you having an affair with Miranda Bloomfeather?'

'No, and No!' he said triumphantly. 'Alice, how could you even think such a thing? Miranda is one of my brighter students, but a mere girl. And you and I have been married for sixteen years! It is obvious that I am committed to the success of our marriage, Alice! Why! Just look at my commitment to the success of our marital counselling! Who was here first today? And who was late, Alice? And who was rude to Mrs Bland?'

Alice goggled at him. 'But you said last night . . .' she started.

Charles sat back in his chair and glanced at Mrs

Bland. Promptly she held up one admonitory finger. 'Stay in the Here and Now, Alice,' she said sweetly. 'How do you feel about what Professor Hartley has said to you *now*?'

'You're lying!' Alice said flatly. 'I know you are having sex with Miranda. And I know you want to end the marriage.'

Charles smiled at her pityingly and shook his head. 'Alice, Alice, Alice,' he said softly. 'It makes me so sad when I see your jealousy drive you out of control like this. You have delusions, Alice. All this is the product of your jealous imagination.'

Alice glared blankly at him and then at Mrs Bland.

She nodded. 'Your husband is right, Alice,' she said. 'You have to work on trusting him. I want you both to come to me for an extra session this week and we will do some exercises around trust. Would Friday morning at this time be possible, Professor?'

Charles reached for his briefcase and made a great play of checking his diary. Neither of them asked if Alice was free. Alice was always free.

'Yes,' he said at length. 'And I think, Mrs Bland, that we should seriously consider whether Alice should have separate therapy sessions to help her cope with her paranoia.'

Mrs Bland nodded, looking thoughtfully at Alice.

'Perhaps even medication,' Charles said softly. 'Perhaps even a period of hospitalization . . .'

Mrs Bland nodded, thoughtful again. Alice, her world whirling around her, listened to her husband making the first moves to have her put away, and could not find the power to protest.

Charles glanced at his watch, and snapped his briefcase shut. 'Before we close I want to ask Alice for an agreement,' he said in a bright, businesslike voice. 'I want my furniture back in my house by the time I come home this evening – and not a scratch or a dent or a chip on anything.'

Alice got up slowly and walked towards the window. From where she stood she could see the blue roof of Michael's pantechnicon. It was like a rebel flag. Her spirits suddenly soared. There lay her freedom, there was the open road away from this claustrophobic room and these two experts. Charles could plan what he wished, Alice was Born Free. With new courage Alice swung around and opened her mouth to claim her freedom, to deny Charles's power, to shriek her defiance.

'Time's up,' said Mrs Bland blandly. No one was ever allowed to prolong the session.

Mrs Bland picked up her pale grey suede music case, shot a quick look at Alice and a longer smile at Charles, and slid unstoppably from the room.

Charles stood up. His smile at Alice was triumphant. 'See you at home tonight, darling,' he said loudly enough for Mrs Bland to hear from the next room where she tidied her paperwork. 'Don't forget our agreement about the furniture.'

He went from the room without another glance at her. Alice stood by the window and watched him go. As he entered the tower block of the Psychology

Department she saw Miranda Bloomfeather in a white miniskirt and high white boots lounge towards him and fall into step beside him.

Alice clutched her skirts in her hands and whirled out of the counselling room, down the stairs and across the lawns to Michael as if she were running for her life.

He was waiting for her in the cab of the van with the engine idling. Alice scuttled across the grass, gathered up her skirts, leaped up into the cab and slammed the door.

'Drive!' Alice yelled. 'Drive, Michael! Let's get outta here!'

Startled, Michael pressed the accelerator and for once did not stall. The engine roared under his inexpert handling, and he swung the wheel around. They drove noisily around the perimeter road of the campus and then turned out of the campus on to the dual carriageway and headed east along the coast.

'All right?' Michael asked over the noise of a driver braking sharply behind them as they wove from slow lane to fast lane and back again.

Alice wound down the window and let the wind ruffle her hair. 'All right now,' she said. 'I have just had a most unpleasant forty minutes.'

Michael glanced at her, surprised. 'I wouldn't have thought anyone could be unpleasant to you,' he said. 'I would have thought you would have been a match for anyone!'

Alice smiled at him and then turned her head and

31

watched the hedges flicker past. A car overtook on the inside, sounding its horn. The driver waved and shouted something. Alice waved pleasantly back.

'Yes,' she said. 'It's odd. I suppose it was an old bad habit.' She paused. 'I think I'll give it up,' she said.

She lay back and closed her eyes, reviewing her marriage as an old bad habit which it was time to give up. Slowly her heartbeat returned to normal. The image of Mrs Bland's conspiracy with Professor Hartley was left behind them. Alice was driving away from the bastion of the Professor's power: his work, the institution of the university, his authority over his students, his control over Alice. Alice could feel the bonds of a lifetime stretching and breaking. She threw back her head and started to hum in the long pulsing column of her white throat.

Michael smiled at her pleasure and changed gear from second to third, the engine screaming for release. A motorcyclist cut in front of them and then felt terror surge as the van leaped forward and chased him from lane to lane across the road as Michael glanced at Alice and swerved to the left, and then turned his attention back to the road and swerved to the right.

It was a pleasant drive in the early-morning sunshine. Grass-like stuff, which Michael vaguely assumed to be wheat, was growing green in the fields. White birds which were probably seagulls were circling behind a lone tractor. On the hills of the Downs the little blobs of white were sheep and the tiny blobs beside them were either very small sheep – perhaps lambs – or dumped copies of the *European*.

Alice wound down the window and the sweet smell of fresh-cut hay blew into the cab. Michael sneezed; Alice inhaled deeply, leaned her head back and closed her eyes. Her face was shining with her joy while her heart still pounded with the throb of adrenalin. Every now and then she exclaimed 'And another thing . . .' and then fell silent. Her hair crackled with static electricity as if it were charged with Alice's newly freed energy.

They drove along the main road, and then turned right down the narrow road to Rithering village. Small birds sang loudly in the hedgerows, the uncut grass of the verges was speckled with flowers which Michael recognized unerringly as daisies of various different shapes, sizes and colours. The hawthorn buds were thick and white in the hedges, apple blossom and cherry blossom snowed petals down on to the lane. Michael thought that the eglantine was probably blowing. He tooted his horn at a particularly sharp corner and waved with the casual friendliness of country folk at the driver coming in the opposite direction who was forced to brake and swerve and run into the ditch.

'Nearly there,' he commented.

Alice opened her eyes and leaned forward to rummage in a large black rucksack at her feet which was lumpy with bottles of medicine and packages of herbs and seeds.

'What have you got in there?' Michael asked curiously.

Alice veiled her eyes with her eyelashes and smiled. 'Nature's cures,' she said. 'I have been a herbalist and a natural healer for many years. If your Aunt is not ready to leave this earthly plane it may be that I have something which might cure her. If she is wanting to make an easy transition to the next plane then I have some herbal teas which will help her on her way.'

'Oh good,' Michael nodded. Then he said suddenly 'What?' and the van swooped perilously close to the bank at the far side of the road as the meaning of her words hit him. 'Help her on her way?' he yelped. 'What d'you mean?'

Alice smiled again, that special smile which denoted that she was in touch with deep elemental forces. It gave Professor Hartley the creeps, but Michael was new to it and it thrilled him down to his toes. His big right toe, less controlled than the others, gave an excited little twitch and the pantechnicon leaped forward.

'Don't worry,' Alice said. And Michael could do nothing but smile back at her.

He had a bit of trouble turning the van into the narrow gateway which was marked with a lopsided sign – Rithering Manor. The furniture clanked and shifted ominously as the van bumped up the pot-holed gravel drive. Low hanging boughs of slowly falling trees banged on the roof of the van and roses run to briar scratched at the windows and the paint-

work. The house itself was dark; it looked uninhab-
ited, standing alone among tall trees on the outskirts
of the village, the high gable ends pointing at a sky
which had grown suddenly cloudy.

Michael stopped the van in front of the house
and went up the shallow steps to the large double
wooden doors, dusty with peeling paint. He pulled
at the bell-knob. It came off in his hand with the
promptness which normally only happens when
these things are arranged by a good special effects
department. He looked back towards the van for
help from Alice.

She shouldered her rucksack and, wrapping an
extra scarf or two around her head, came up the
steps.

'Try the door,' she advised.

It yielded at once to his touch. Feeling for Alice's
hand, Michael stepped over the threshold into the
darkness of the hall.

'Who's that?' came a voice. A strong and hearty
male voice from the front room on their left.

'It's Michael!' squeaked Michael. He got a firm
grip of himself and tightened his hold on Alice's
hand. 'Michael Coulter,' he said. This time he had
gone too far in the other direction. He sounded as if
he were auditioning for the bass part in *Figaro*.
'I've come to see my Aunt,' he said in a pitch
midway between the squeak and basso profundo.
'My Aunt, Miss Sarah Coulter.'

'You've left it a bit late,' came the reply. The
door opened and a thick-set, grey-haired man stood

35

in the doorway looking them over. 'She's dead. Are you the lad from the university?'

'I am her nephew, Michael,' said Michael, trying for a little dignity.

'And you must be Mrs Coulter?'

Alice flushed scarlet with pleasure at being mistaken for Michael's wife. Michael's grip on her hand tightened. It was a tender moment for them both.

'I didn't know you were staying with your son or I'd have contacted you direct, Mrs Coulter,' the man said.

Alice's flush went redder but she abruptly lost her smile. 'I am a friend of Michael's,' she said icily. 'I came over with him today to keep him company.'

'Oh aye,' the man nodded. 'Well I'm Doctor Simmonds, I sent the message to you. I'm afraid you're too late. She's dead.'

'Oh,' Michael said blankly. 'Oh dear.'

Alice put the rucksack sulkily down on the tiled hall floor. A large green-eyed, thick-coated black cat came out of the shadows and sniffed at it.

'I've just written out the death certificate,' the doctor said cheerfully. 'Natural causes of course. She was eighty-eight. I think it was the Beaujolais Nouveau, I warned her not to drink it after Christmas but she was always stubborn.

'I'll send the undertakers around later. But they won't be able to fit her in for at least a couple of days. She'll be all right here as long as it doesn't get too hot.'

Michael gulped, his face went greenish in the shadowy hall.

'You're the only heir, you know,' the doctor said chattily. He came out of the sitting-room with his black bag, waving the death certificate to dry the ink. 'I see you brought your things to move in at once. Bit precipitate of you I would have thought; but young people today have very little sense of etiquette.'

Alice's grip on Michael's hand tightened.

'Anyway, I'll leave you to unload,' he said cheerily. 'Don't block up the hall with anything till they've got the coffin out.' He paused for a moment. 'We'll be neighbours,' he said without much pleasure. 'It's a quiet village this; expensive. We like it like that.' He looked hard at Michael's young gormless face and then glanced at Alice's flowing bright gown and coloured scarves. 'Nothing that brings down property prices will be tolerated in this village,' he said abruptly. 'No hippies *here* thank you. G'day!'

His confident footsteps echoed on the loose tiles of the hall. Alice and Michael stood in silence, still hand-clasped. The big black cat backed up to Alice's bag of herbal remedies and shot a spray of yellow urine directly and accurately all over it.

There was a long silence. Not even the hissing noise of the peeing cat distracted Michael and Alice from their thoughts.

'Should we see her?' Michael asked in a hushed tone.

Alice nodded. She went towards the uncarpeted stairs and led the way, one hand trailing along the sticky banister, the treads of the stairs creaking beneath each step. The stairs swept around a half-landing beneath a cobwebby high window and then arrived at the main landing. To left and right were doors closed on empty bedrooms, the door to the master bedroom was straight ahead. It stood open. Alice crossed the threshold and then paused.

The old lady was dressed in a perfectly white nightgown with a nightcap tied neatly around her white head. She was propped high on clean white pillows trimmed with lace. She looked like everyone's idea of a sweetly dead old lady. She looked like Whistler's Mother; only supine. On her bedside table were two empty bottles of Beaujolais Nouveau, and on the coverlet of her bed were price lists from wine merchants and yesterday's *Sporting Life*.

Alice started to hum, a deep rhythmic buzz of sound from the back of her throat like a massive, tuneful bee. She went over to the sash window and flung it up to welcome the sunshine into the shaded room. Michael, who dimly remembered seeing Alice hurling furniture from the spare bedroom window the night before, shot an anxious look at her as if she might be planning to toss Aunty Sarah out into the rose beds. But Alice was communing with the forces of Nature and freeing Aunty Sarah's aura and essence and incorporeal body to mingle with the warm sunshine and be transported to a higher plane.

'Hummm . . .' she droned.

Michael dipped his head in an awkward little bow to the still figure in the bed and stepped softly out of the room. From his previous visit he thought he remembered that the kitchen was at the back of the house. He had not eaten since yesterday afternoon, and last night had been the most active of his life. He badly wanted a cup of coffee. He was also thinking that he should telephone his parents at once and tell them of Aunty Sarah's death and his rich inheritance. Michael's brain, under-fed and over-excited, spun with dreams and hopes.

The kitchen was as immaculate as Aunty Sarah's bedroom. Michael filled the kettle and put it on to boil, noting that Aunty Sarah's cleaner had let the rest of the house accumulate dust as long as the kitchen, Aunty Sarah's room and the bathroom were as perfect as they had been in the roaring twenties when Aunty Sarah's exacting standards had been set.

Just as the kettle was boiling, Alice came in.

She was wearing her dreamy look which sent a shiver of anticipation down Michael's spine.

'Tea, if there is any,' she said with flute-like sweetness. 'Coffee is a poison, you know, Michael.'

Michael nodded obediently, and looked for the canister of tea instead.

'So you are the heir?' she asked.

Michael nodded. 'I always knew I would be,' he said. 'But I didn't really think about it. She was one of those old ladies who look like they will live forever, you know.'

He warmed the pot and made the tea. There was fresh milk in the fridge. Alice frowned as he put the bottle on the table. Michael looked for a milk jug and poured it in, but that seemed to make it no better.

'Milk is a poison, you know, Michael,' she said.

'Oh.' Michael had not known this. He had drunk milk seldom after leaving primary school where he had to finish up one of those little bottles every break-time before he was allowed out to play. He had not liked the stuff much then, and he had a squeamish loathing for the skin on custard or hot chocolate; but he would not have called it poison exactly. However, he was unlikely to oppose Alice on this matter, or any other. He drank his tea black and sugarless. He did not think it was worth trying for the sugar bowl.

'What will you do?' Alice asked. She finished her tea and was peering into the depths of her cup. 'What do you plan to do with this house?'

Michael gazed longingly at her. Blinkie, unseen in Michael's baggy trousers, reared up and gazed longingly at her too.

'I don't know,' Michael said weakly. 'It depends, I suppose.'

Alice's eyes when she looked up from her cup were so misty that he was afraid she had scalded them with the steam. 'Depends on what?' she asked, her voice silky.

Michael opened his mouth. All that came out was a pathetic squeak, wordless.

Alice rose to her feet; she was humming as she had done in Aunty Sarah's bedroom but this time the noise was more insistent, like the distant purr of a lawn-mower in an enthusiast's garden. Slowly but surely she unwound one of the scarves at her throat and held it across her face. Above the gauzy top her dark eyes stared hypnotically at Michael.

Her feet traced strange patterns on the flagstones of the kitchen floor. Michael crossed his legs in an effort to keep Blinkie aligned with at least some part of his body. She danced around in a little circle then she stood still and shivered her body in a sinuous snake-like tremble which set all the little beads and bells and discs on her scarves trembling and ringing.

This was unfortunate. The cat, mistaking the noise for the welcome clatter of the tin-opener, came running into the kitchen and seeing there was nothing in his bowl let out a contemptuous bawl of disapproval. Alice ignored him completely and took one small step towards Michael.

Michael pushed his chair back. He knew he was grinning in a village-idiotish sort of way but he could not manage his facial muscles at the same time as keeping everything else still.

Alice shimmered with more energy, her rounded breasts vibrating freely behind the kaftan. Michael, who had a vivid recollection from last night of lying beneath Alice and heading first one perfect globe and then another like a wet-dreaming soccer star, gave his familiar wail of despair, collapsed head first on the kitchen table and gave up his essence once more – before Alice had dropped more than one scarf.

Alice rested her face against his heaving shoulders and inhaled deeply. Though the essences slapped lightly into the tension areas of neck and around the eyes is best of all, the aura of yin is deeply restorative too. And, on a lower but none the less significant plane, it was a long time since anyone had shown much interest before veil number twelve.

As they embraced thus, in silent communion, the tom cat came a little closer and sniffed at Alice's bare feet. She looked down at him with her dark eyes.

The cat looked back.

Alice knew herself to be in touch with Nature and the Life Force in all its manifestations; she sensed the cat responding to that Force in her.

The cat's green eyes gazed inscrutably into Alice's black ones. Anyone watching them would almost have believed that they were speaking to each other. Alice felt the hairs on the back of her neck prickle as she sensed the cat willing her to understand something. Her fingertips prickled as their auras brushed, overlapped, mingled.

The cat dropped its eyes first, turned from Alice, and then hesitated. Alice waited, unmoving, for whatever gesture the cat might make. Slowly and solemnly, the cat backed up and with its usual accuracy pissed all over the hem of Alice's kaftan, her bare right leg, and her right sandal with the little bells on the straps.

Alice gasped for a moment with shock and irritation but then exhaled deeply to bring herself under
control. She released Michael and stepped away
from him, saying nothing, though her right foot was
warm and wet. Michael, still slightly shaky, sat up
and poured himself another cup of sour tea.

'That cat is blocking my Life Force,' Alice said.
Her voice was mellow and strong. 'He has a negative
presence. Can you feel it?'

Michael shook his head, the round lenses of his
glasses fixed trustingly on Alice's face.

'His aura is dark,' Alice said certainly. 'His magnetic field is distorted.'

Michael looked at the cat, which was now sitting
in a patch of sunlight washing his private parts with
his back leg casually hitched over his shoulder and
the air of a good job well done.

'He may have fleas,' Michael offered. 'Aunty
Sarah said he had when I was last here.'

Alice nodded. 'She would have sensed that
he was flawed,' she said. 'His Life Force is very
weak.'

Alice went to the back door of the kitchen and
opened it. Sunlight flooded on to the kitchen floor,
illuminating Alice's one wet footprint dot-and-carry-
ing across the flagstones. Michael looked at it without curiosity.

'Cat!' Alice called peremptorily. The cat looked
up at her and went trustingly towards her. Alice
stepped out of Michael's line of sight into the
garden, the cat close behind her. There was a yowl

of anger and dismay which was suddenly cut abruptly short. Alice came back into the kitchen with her wide-hipped swaying pace. She was trailing the limp cat by the tail, as lesser women trail mink coats. There was a dustbin by the door; she slung the cat into it and clanged the lid, then came back to sit down at the table.

'I knew his Life Force was weak,' she said conversationally to Michael.

Michael, dumbstruck, nodded; gulped his tea. His teeth clattered a little on the rim of his cup. They sat in the silence of satisfied lovers for a little while.

'So what will you do with this house?' Alice asked again.

Michael took a deep breath. 'I wonder if I could live here while I finish my degree,' he said. 'I've never liked living in Hall. I could live here and rent some of the rooms.'

Alice looked down into the bottom of her cup.

'May I tell you what I see?' she asked.

Michael nodded.

'I can see a place of growth here, of regeneration, of rebirth.' She took his cup from his nerveless hands and clasped them in her own. 'We could live here, you and I,' she said, her voice husky with power. 'We could run it as a growth centre, for people to try alternative medicine, alternative life-styles.' Her tongue flicked swiftly across her lips. 'Therapies,' she said. 'Water therapy, mud therapy . . . sexual therapy, Michael.'

She glanced at him. 'It's a perfect place,' she said. 'Privacy, large rooms, an air of convincing elegance. We could do it. We could do it together, Michael.'

Michael gasped. He had been caught up by the soothing repetition of her voice into thinking she was telling his fortune. But it was more than that! It was an offer, a partnership. Him and Mrs Hartley! Together forever!

Gosh!

'I don't know anything about alternative life-styles,' he said. He sounded feeble, even to himself. Especially to himself.

Alice shrugged. 'You could go on courses,' she said. 'You could go on retreats. I would teach you everything I know. You are sensitive, Michael. You know Yourself. The moment I saw your aura I knew you were one of those who Know. One of those who don't have to learn everything from sim-plistic textbooks, who don't have to have everything taught and written down.

'Little bits of paper and examinations,' she said bitterly, thinking of Miranda Bloomfeather and her A-minus. 'Libraries of bits of paper, mountains of useless facts. You either instinctively know some-thing or you do not. All the rest is just bureaucracy.'

Michael heaved a great sigh of longing. He was, after all, a student approaching the final examina-tions of a three-year course upon which the suc-cess of the rest of his life would depend. It is a time when everyone feels a natural repugnance for

academic information, and the appeal of an instinc-
tive knowledge which can be learned without effort
is particularly high.

'Do you think we could do it?' he asked longingly.

'I Feel we could do it,' she replied, condemning
thought to bureaucracy as well. 'I Know we could
do it. I See it!'

'Yes! Oh Yes!'cried Michael. Blinkie, as if wak-
ened from a doze by their raised voices, lifted his
head. Michael got up as well and took Alice by the
hand. He thought if he was very, very quick, and
thought very hard all the time about Henry James's
literary technique in – say – *The Turn of the Screw*
– No! not that word! Not that! in say – *The Ambassa-
dors* – he might be able to get Alice's kaftan up and
his jeans down before Alice's clever hands went
down and drew his essences into her cupped palms
instead of the place where he would really much
rather they went.

'Yes!' he cried, nearing his goal as Alice obligingly
sank to the stone floor. He captured both her hands
and held them above her head. Alice, though mourning the loss of male essence for the tension areas of
her epidermis, could not help but writhe in delight
at being held with such dominance. And on a cold
stone floor too! It really was too At One for words
when . . .

SUDDENLY THERE WAS A DREADFUL HAMMERING NOISE ON THE CEILING!

'My God what's that!' cried Michael, leaping to his feet. Blinkie dived back inside his trousers like a seal off a rock in stormy weather.

Alice scrambled to her feet and gazed wildly around her. The noise came from upstairs where there was nothing, could be nothing, but the stiffening mortal remains of Aunty Sarah.

'Daisy!' A sharp old voice, sharp as a cracked bell, echoed down through the empty house. 'Daisy! Where's my brandy and egg-nog? Daisy! You lazy bitch! Bring it up at once!'

Michael was blanched white with superstitious terror.

'That's Aunty Sarah's voice,' he quavered, reaching instinctively for Alice. She brushed past him and went to fetch her rucksack from the hall. She poured out the contents in an avalanche of alternatives on to the wide kitchen table.

'She's coming through from the Other Side,' she muttered. 'It would be the essences which drew her, my sensitivity and your essences. If I can create the right ambience ...' One little jar after another she drew towards her, selecting, rejecting, then she spread out her kaftan like a peasant girl's apron and loaded them in.

'Upstairs!' she hissed to Michael, her dark eyes blazing with excitement. 'Upstairs! With a manifestation this strong we may even see her! The dear old lady!'

Michael lagged unwillingly behind as Alice ran light-footed up the stairs, her bottles clinking in her

47

kaftan. She strode into the bedroom and fell back, in shock.

Aunty Sarah was sitting up in bed, hammering on the floor with a silver-handled ebony stick. 'Who the hell are you?' she demanded as Alice abruptly halted on the threshold. 'Where's my morning tea? Where's my newspaper? Where's my brandy and egg-nog? And why isn't Daisy here? If you're a temporary you can just go straight back to Lithuania or wherever you've come from. I won't have au pairs and they all know it!'

'Aunty Sarah,' Michael popped his head around Alice, 'Aunty Sarah, do you know me?'

Her bright gaze swept him pityingly. 'Of course I do,' she said. 'You're my nephew, that idiot Michael Coulter.'

'Oh good,' said Michael weakly. 'And Aunty,' he said tentatively, 'are you feeling quite all right?'

'Of course I am!' she snapped. 'I'm half dead of hunger and thirst, but I'm all right! Where is Daisy with my tea? Fetch her at once!'

'Did you say half dead, Aunty?' Michael asked cunningly, trying to lure Aunty Sarah on to some common ground. 'Did you say half dead?'

'God give me peace,' she exclaimed to the ceiling. 'I'd rather be half dead than halfwitted. Michael! Go downstairs at once, and tell Daisy to come up here and bring me my tea and my brandy. Take this awful woman with you. She's obviously one of those au pairs from the agency who can't speak a word of English. Here!' This was directly to Alice who still stood, frozen, her kaftan loaded with herbs and oils which were to aid communication with the other world, her head still full of dreams of an alternative lifestyle and a young lover. 'Here! Heidi! Go away! Gotterdammerung! or whatever. Skit! Skedaddle! And send up Daisy to me.'

Michael stepped backwards, he laid hold of one of Alice's floating scarves and tweaked it gently. Without a word she let him reverse her from the room which they had entered so blithely with such high hopes of astral communication.

All gone.

All gone.

And nothing left but a bad-tempered old lady who looked, as Michael had so rightly said earlier, as if she would live, occupying this perfect alternative therapy centre, forever.

They slumped side by side at the kitchen table. Alice listlessly took up one of her jars of herbs.

There was another abrupt banging on the ceiling.

'And bring up Thomas my cat!' yelled Aunty Sarah. 'Where is he? I want Thomas!'

Alice and Michael exchanged one appalled look and then found their eyes drawn irresistibly towards the dustbin. Neither of them would have been in the least surprised if the lid had risen and Thomas also had returned miraculously to this material plane.

They waited a few moments.

Nothing happened.

Michael, exercising some manly courage, went across the kitchen floor, which was still puddled with Thomas's final act, lifted the bin lid and looked in.

At least the cat was still dead.

'What will you do?' Alice murmured dully.

Michael shrugged his shoulders. 'I suppose I shall go and find Doctor Simmonds,' he said. 'He'll have to come back and see her. He'll know where Daisy lives. She's in one of the houses in the village but I don't know which one. I'll ring up my Dad and tell him Aunty Sarah's been ill. I'll drive us back to campus. The van's got to be back at midday. Where shall I take your furniture?'

Alice looked at him blankly. The alternative therapy centre was fading so fast that Michael had almost forgotten it already. All there was for her in the future might be an occasional share of his narrow bed in the little room, and the nightly wheezes of her husband as his fevered imagination placed him and Miranda Bloomfeather in more and more exotic locations and in foreign countries too. There would be the grisly support and sympathy of her women friends. There would be interminable counselling sessions in which Alice would be made to feel obscurely to blame and clearly in the wrong. There would be a long, hopeless seeking through esoteric and unlikely therapy, for such scant legal fun is available to a forty-year-old woman whose husband despises her. Alice knew that without regular sex and lots of essence her neck would go crepey. She did not need a spiritual guide or a tarot reading to recognize the chance of a lifetime when it came on a plate.

She rose to her feet.

There was another banging on the ceiling. 'If Daisy is not up here in five minutes with my tea and my brandy and my cat I shall dock ten shillings off her wages,' came the ringing voice.

Alice's eyes hardened. Her mouth was set. 'Your Aunty Sarah is a negative Life Force,' she said firmly.

Michael's eyes goggled behind the round lenses.

'She has a bad aura,' Alice said. 'Her magnetic field is distorted. She is trying to fight her destiny. She has a weak Life Force. She is ready to Go Over.'

Michael tried to speak but found his voice had gone. 'What d'you mean?' he whispered.

Alice had turned her back on him. She was switching on the kettle and fetching a clean cup and saucer from the Welsh dresser.

'She has a negative Life Force,' she said quietly. 'She needs help to be At One with her destiny – her move to another plane.'

The kettle boiled. Alice picked up the tea caddy and spooned tea into the pot. She added boiling water. She put the teapot on the tray with the milk jug and the sugar bowl. Then she took a slim dark bottle and measured four precise drops of a clear odourless liquid into the teapot.

'I'm giving her a nice herbal tea,' she said.

Michael leaped to his feet but became entangled with the table leg. By the time he was free of the furniture Alice was carrying the tray upstairs, her face Madonna-like in its serenity.

'Please don't, Mrs Hartley!' he cried. 'Please don't give her a herbal tea, Mrs Hartley. It's much better not! Please not a herbal tea, Mrs Hartley!'

Aunty Sarah was sitting up in bed scowling at a handsome gold hunter watch when Alice and Michael tumbled into the room, Alice holding the tray and looking determined, Michael with a frightened grip on one of her trailing shawls.

'Thought I'd told *you* to get lost,' the old lady said acerbically. 'What's that?' she demanded, pointing to the tray. 'And where's Daisy?'

'Daisy's not here today,' Alice said in a confident tone. She put down the tray on the bedside table and nodded pleasantly at Aunty Sarah. 'I'm a friend of Michael's,' she said. 'Your doctor sent a message to say you weren't well so we both came over to see you. I shall look after you until Daisy arrives.'

'Oh,' the old lady said, unconvinced. She shot a look at Alice's flowing kaftan and the scarves with the glittery coins. 'Not one of them Harry Krishners, are you?'

'No,' Alice said levelly. She reached over and poured the tea into the cup. 'Milk? Sugar?'

'No sugar,' the old lady said, irritated at the suggestion. 'Not one of the Mormons? Seventh Day Adventists? Quakers? Anarchists? Socialists?'

'I have no god but the Great Earth Mother,' Alice said calmly. 'Drink your tea, Aunty Sarah.'

'Miss Coulter to you,' she replied instantly and with malice. She dipped her puckered old face towards the teacup. Michael held his breath, about to cry out, about to dash the cup from her hand.

She paused. 'Not from the Welfare?' she asked sharply. 'Housing? Social Services? Not one of those little-Miss-Nosey-Parker-social-workers come to see if I'm dying in my bed, are you?'

'No,' Alice said steadily. 'Just a friend of Michael's from the university.'

'Don't drink the tea,' Michael said in a whisper too soft to be heard by anyone but his own quivering ears and feeble conscience.

Aunty Sarah puckered up her dry pale lips, readying herself to drink. 'Not a neighbourhood watch scheme?' she said with sudden suspicion. 'Not come to befriend me? Not Friends of the Aged? Not want to understand me?'

'No,' Alice said, her voice no less patient.

'Senile Dementia Support Group!' Aunty Sarah screeched. She pointed a quivering bony finger accusingly. 'You've come to talk through my confusions with me!'

'Not at all,' Alice said. She gleamed at the old lady. 'I've come to poison you with herbal tea so that Michael can inherit this house and he and I can live here forever.'

'Noommmiiimmmmpppp!' Michael moaned.

Aunty Sarah cackled like an old witch. 'That's good!' she said delightedly. 'I love a good joke. I like you!' She took a deep swig of tea. 'I like you, Heidi! You've got spirit!' She gulped swiftly.

'DON'T DRINK THE TEA!' Michael said

clearly. He stepped into the centre of the room, from behind Alice's cascade of skirts. He snatched the cup from Aunty Sarah's hands with all the power of a young man who has found the deep secret source of potency inside himself. Michael had read D. H. Lawrence and he recognized the feeling welling up inside him. He was as male and as powerful as a bull in a meadow. He was strong like the dark primeval soil. He was thrusting like an oak tree reaching towards light. He was free of the pathetic chains of bourgeois society, his face glowed, he breathed deeply into his pouter-pigeon chest. He was a man who has faced a very great temptation and managed to spurn it. Hearing Alice speak of murder and hearing poor old Aunty Sarah laugh so trustingly had broken Michael's reserve. His innocence had gone. In its place was strength.

'Aunty Sarah, I Forbid You To Drink That Tea,' he said. Then he looked from the perfectly empty cup to the little old lady. 'Oh dear,' he said.

'We'll leave you to have a little rest now,' Alice said sweetly. She picked up the tray again and put it in Michael's nerveless hands. 'If you want anything, just call. I shall stay in earshot, for the next few minutes.'

'Mmmmnnnniiiiinnnn?' said Michael.

'Just ten minutes,' Alice confirmed. She took Michael gently by the shoulders and propelled him gently from the room. 'Ten minutes, and so peaceful, Michael. And the death certificate already made out to natural causes, and the doctor been.'

At the word 'death' Michael's feet entangled themselves and he came to an abrupt standstill on the top step.

Alice took his little head in her hands and turned his face towards hers. Her dark eyes were luminous, her lips moist. When she spoke he could feel the warmth of her breath on his face.

'Michael,' she said softly, 'I really do hope you are At One with your destiny?'

Under the shimmery kaftan her breasts were rounded and warm. Michael *knew* this to be a fact and it did not help his breathing.

His knuckles whitened as his grip tightened on the handles of the tray and the milk jug went 'chink chink chink chink' against the teapot.

'Mmmmmiiiinnnn!' he said.

'*I* am At One with my destiny, Michael,' she said. 'I believe my destiny is you. We met only last night yet already we have thoughts in common, we have our minds attuned, we have made passionate, abandoned love, and we have killed a boring old lady and gained a substantial property ideal for Family Home or conversion to Small Business Premises, in a highly desirable village within Easy Commuting Distance of London or Brighton.'

She took the tray from his slackened grip and put it down softly on the parquet floor of the landing.

'Touch me, Michael!' she urged. Michael stuck out both his hands feebly, like PC Plod directing Toytown traffic. His flat hands thumped comfortingly on her rounded breasts. Michael revolved them stiffly in a clockwise motion. Alice moaned and dropped to the floor, sitting warmly and heavily on his feet, clasping her arms around his knees which meant that her head pressed, pressed, pressed . . .

Blinkie, who had been quiescent since his fright in the kitchen, pressed with increasing urgency in reply. For one demented moment Michael wanted to take him out and give him a good talking to. He was in league with Mrs Hartley and had been since they had first met. Now she was pressing . . . and he was pressing . . . and . . . Michael moaned softly and as his knees buckled beneath him tumbled on the stairs beside Mrs Hartley.

'Every modern convenience,' she said softly as she unzipped his trousers with casual skill, one hand only. Michael cried out softly, and scrabbled for purchase on the uncarpeted stairs like a mountaineer who has forgotten his crampons. He entered her at last with a grunt of triumph, and a tight grip on the uprights of the banister.

'With all traditional features retained, only in need of sympathetic redecoration,' Mrs Hartley murmured as her eyelids fluttered shut in ecstasy.

Michael's Aunty may have called him. She may have called upon her Maker, she may have called on the Angel Gabriel and he may have replied with a chorus of heavenly hallelujahs! Michael, for one, was deaf to everything for long moments. When he came to himself the ten minutes which Alice had predicted had passed. Michael and Alice lay on the stairs still and silent. Aunty in her bedroom was pretty quiet too.

'Is she . . .?' Michael asked as he came to and noted the unearthly stillness of the house.

Alice nodded solemnly. She stood up, brushed down her gown and went towards the bedroom. 'Hummmmm . . .' she started.

Michael, fascinated, aghast, followed her into the bedroom. Aunty Sarah was propped up on the pillows as usual. A slight smile curved her mouth, her eyes were shut. The bedroom was quiet and sunny.

'There,' Alice said with an air of quiet satisfaction. 'That's done. Now we must get the things out of the removal van. You said you had to get it back at midday.'

Michael gulped and nodded. He had a strong suspicion, compounded by lack of food and excessive sexual pleasure, that his brain had exploded and was whirling in outer space. He followed Alice downstairs without a murmur and once more took the other end of Professor Hartley's wardrobe and then his bed and then his chest of drawers, the crated box of his nick-nacks, the mirror in its heavy gilt frame, the coat-stand which would look nice in the hall, the Afghan rugs.

In the middle of it all Alice pounced on her diary which was poking out from a tea chest filled with peasant woodwork.

'There it is!' she said, pleased. 'Now I can really start! You carry on, darling, I shan't be a mo!'

She vanished then, into the sitting-room, and Michael could hear her, every time he staggered through the hall with another box, or with another dining-room chair, dialling and talking, dialling and talking. Once he caught a snippet of the conversation: 'Oh dahling!' she said in a voice he had not heard before. 'We had it all wrong! All! All wrong! All that dreary trouble trying to understand them! All those seminars about Empty Nest Syndrome, and the Academic Wife, and What Tenure Means to Your Man, and the impact of stress on male libido. All wrong!' She was silent for a moment and then she chuckled richly and warmly. 'Miranda Bloomfeather?' she said. 'All that means nothing to me now. I am free. I have liberated myself.' The telephone crackled urgently. Alice chuckled again. 'I won't tell you over the phone, it's too exciting,' she said. 'Come around this evening and I'll tell all of you then. Bring everyone! Everyone!'

Then Michael heard her hang up and dial again.

Michael carried on humping furniture while Alice's voice went on in the sitting-room until the pantechnicon was empty. Then, as he heaved the last thing – a well-padded footstool – into the sitting-room, she broke off from the phone.

'Why darling, you look quite pale,' she said. 'Are you all right?'

Michael sat down heavily on one of Professor Hartley's chesterfield armchairs. 'Ummmmlummmph,' he said.

Alice frowned very slightly looking at Michael's

white sweaty face. She smothered a sigh of irritation waiting for him to speak. Michael looked silently back at her. Aunty Sarah, upstairs, looked nowhere at nothing. Michael was not absolutely sure that he was having a good time.

Alice stepped back a pace to see him more fully. She absorbed once more his fluffy halo of curly hair, his innocent moon-like round spectacles, the endearing shape of his mouth, his slight, nervous body, and his delicious youth.

'Oh, darling,' she said lovingly. 'You must be exhausted. Why don't you stay right there while I make us some lunch?'

'There's no food in the house, I looked,' Michael said sulkily.

Alice gave a rippling, joyful laugh. 'Silly boy! There's all the food in my freezer, and in my fridge! Cakes, soups, stews, roasts, all sorts. I'll have a good meal on the table in thirty minutes! You'll see!'

Michael's downward pout turned upwards into a smile. Alice darted into the kitchen and he could hear the hum of Professor Hartley's deluxe microwave as it switched on to defrost Professor Hartley's nut casserole. Alice came out into the hall again with a little glass in her hand half filled with a pale, golden-brown liquid.

She smiled at Michael with a strange detached smile. 'Have this, darling,' she said encouragingly. 'You'll feel ever so much better.'

Michael let out a shriek of pure terror and

bunched up foetus-like into the furthest corner of the chair. 'Not a herbal tea!' he stammered. 'Please, Mrs Hartley! Not a herbal tea! I feel fine! I feel great! Yeah! My life force is really strong, Mrs Hartley! I am full of positive energy! My aura is . . . is . . . is bristling, Mrs Hartley! Really it is! Look!' Michael vaulted over the back of the armchair and jumped up and down on the spot waving his arms in frantic windmilling motions. 'I just needed a quick breather!' he shouted at the top of his voice. 'Just a moment to restore the life force and now it's great. Gosh! Yes! I really feel full of positive energy, I'm not draining you! Gosh no! I'm really full of life force. Really positive life force!'

Alice stared in bewilderment, as Michael dropped to the floor and started doing feverish press-ups. 'Oh, I feel great!' he puffed. 'Just great! Watch me go! Hey! Mrs Hartley? Hey! Hey! Hey! Mrs Hartley!'

Alice smiled vaguely and nodded. When Michael subsided gasping to the floor, his face flushed, she silently handed him the glass. Michael knew he was going to have to take it.

'What is it?' he asked in a tiny voice. His face puckered. 'Why do I have to drink it?'

'It's Harvey's Luncheon Dry sherry,' Alice said. 'I'm having one in the kitchen, I thought you might like a glass.'

THURSDAY AFTERNOON

The undertakers came after lunch to measure up Aunty Sarah for her coffin. Alice let them in and took them upstairs, Michael stayed in the kitchen brooding over a glass of Professor Hartley's best Cabernet Sauvignon. He heard ominous sounds of moving furniture from upstairs but he felt incapable of action. Whatever was happening would probably be finished by the time he got there, and anyway Alice knew best. The nut casserole lay in a comforting indigestible weight in his stomach. Professor Hartley would have been irritable with wind, but Michael was a young man and the weight of indigestible carbohydrate in his gut reminded him comfortingly of his mother. He dozed.

'All done,' Alice said brightly. She handed him a cup of tea (Brooke Bond) and Michael drank it trustingly, without sniffing. 'They measured her up and they've gone. I didn't want to disturb you so I ordered a pine coffin with brass handles. I get very good resonances from pine. I thought she'd like it.'

Michael nodded. 'Thank you,' he said.

'I had them move her,' Alice said. 'I had them move her across the landing to the spare bedroom, that was the noise. I wanted us to have the master bedroom and I thought you might not like to use her bed.'

Michael nodded emphatically. He would not have liked to use her bed.

'So we're in the master bedroom with my bed and furniture, and she's in her bed in the spare room,' Alice said. 'They couldn't say when they could collect her. She looks very peaceful.' She tapped her teeth with the tip of one rosy nail. 'Much better than before,' she said. 'That doctor isn't up to much. I hate a professional man who leaves a job unfinished.'

Michael nodded. 'What's the time?' he asked.

Alice glanced at Professor Hartley's expensive brass clock, a present from his colleagues in the Psychology Association to mark his year as Chairman.

'Half two,' she said.

'Gosh,' Michael said. 'I have to get that van back.'

'I'll come too,' Alice said. 'We could get my car at the same time. We'll need a car out here.'

For the first time that day Michael glowed with a sense of things coming right.

'All right,' he said nonchalantly. 'What sort of car is it?'

'Only an old Jaguar,' Alice said dismissively. 'But it's very reliable.'

Michael's temporary glow of confidence cooled abruptly. 'A silver-grey one?' he asked.

Alice was winding a couple of scarves around her head; she nodded.

'I think I've seen it,' Michael said miserably.

He had indeed seen it. He had seen it parked in the staff car park at Suffix University. He had seen Professor Hartley parking it and then dusting it off after the exertion of the half-mile drive from home to car park. It was Professor Hartley's pride and joy. He took it to Jaguar car shows and exhibitions. He won prizes with it. He had his picture in the Jaguar car owners' magazine lovingly smiling at it, like a mother whose baby has won the Bonny Baby Contest against keen competition. When he was teaching a seminar of more than an hour he could be seen wrapping it in its own, initialled, little blue tent so that no passing birds could take advantage of his absence and defile it.

'It's got a burglar alarm,' he said. Every student at the university knew that if they heard the expensive hooting which indicated that someone had brushed past Professor Hartley's car and activated the alarm, they were to run at once, at once, to Psych II and tell the Professor that his car was crying for him.

Alice smiled. 'I know the code,' she said smugly.

Despite a lingering anxiety about the Professor's Jaguar car and a tendency to stand up in order to steer the furniture van around corners, Michael enjoyed the drive into Brighton. He had a sense of adventure, of freedom, and a dawning realization that he had gained in the past twenty-four hours: a large and beautiful house, a woman (ditto), and a great deal of tasteful and expensive furniture.

'I don't see why I should finish my degree,' he said. 'It hardly seems worthwhile now.'

Alice was the wife of an academic and had a third-class degree herself. 'Of course you must finish it,' she said firmly.

'But . . .' Michael said.

Alice glanced at him, smiling. 'I'll help you, darling,' she said sweetly. 'And it's so nice to have letters after your name when you're writing to people to complain about things which break down when they're out of guarantee.'

'It's just that I'm not sure about English Literature,' Michael said weakly.

Alice's own degree had been in Biology so she nodded understandingly. She knew that Arts people often had these uncertainties. 'You're not supposed to be sure,' she said. 'You're *supposed* to question. That's how you come to your understanding of the Arts. It's not like doing it with frogs.'

'Doing it with what?' Michael puzzled. He stood up for a corner, and sat down again. Sometimes he could not understand Alice at all.

'Doing it with frogs,' she repeated simply.

'Oh . . . frogs!' Michael said, as if that explained anything. He still had no idea that she had taken her degree in Biology.

He braked, and turned cautiously into the university car park. Behind them some fool careered on to the hard shoulder, fighting for control of his car in an effort to avoid the van.

'I said I'd leave the van at the drama centre,' Michael said glancing, too late, at the rear-view mirror. The road behind them was empty, the crash had occurred on their nearside where Michael would never see it. Like many drivers, Michael was completely indifferent to his wing mirrors, using them only as guiding points as to the width of the vehicle.

Alice gathered up her skirts and shawls as they drove past the faculty car park. 'Drop me off here then,' she said. 'I'll pick up the car and come around to collect you.'

Michael lost his brief moment of confidence. 'Won't he be rather . . . rather . . . upset?' he asked. His voice came out slight and high. He cleared his throat and tried again. This time he bellowed like a bull moose in the rutting season. 'Won't he be angry?'

Alice smiled, showing her white even teeth. 'He'll be epileptic,' she said contentedly. 'But he won't know anything about it until we have gone. Now run along, Michael, I'll meet you outside the drama centre in five minutes.'

She slammed the door. Michael hesitated for one indecisive moment. Then he let in the clutch and pulled away. He saw her turn and stride towards the car park where the hummocky blue canvas shroud of Professor Hartley's concourse-condition

Jaguar billowed in the light summer breeze. Michael braked and paused for a moment, watching Alice in the clear distancing frame of his rear-view mirror. He watched the way she approached the car with her confident swaying stride, the way she untied the straps of the cover from the shining bumpers, skinning the car as easily as a gourmet popping prawns.

A movement in front of Michael made him jump and look forward. It was Professor Hartley like a scarecrow of doom in his dark academic gown, walking slowly and purposefully with his heavy grown-up tread towards his errant wife who, intent on her task, did not even look up.

'Afternoon, Michael,' he said as he went past the cab.

Michael goggled. The Professor, of course, had no idea of the part played by Michael in the midnight stripping of his home, in the early-morning stripping of his wife. The Professor was descending upon his adulterous wife without an idea that her young lover was gawping in his rear-view mirror, a feeble and terrorized bystander to the drama of life.

But Michael was an indecisive, inexperienced youth no more. Michael had been Mrs Hartley's lover. Michael's heart had beaten with the deep rhythms of the earth. Michael had made love (or at any rate very nearly) on a stone floor. Michael had been accessory to murder, partner in adultery, accomplice in fraud. He did not hesitate for a moment.

He let in the clutch as softly as a ballet dancer

performing the *pas de cheval*, and sweetly, almost silently, drove away.

He waited outside the drama centre, as he had been told to do, like an apprentice knight unkindly ordered to face west and wait for the sun to rise before him by jovial time-served knights, who would in later incarnations send lads to the company stores with instructions to ask for 'a long stand'. But he waited without hope. He saw too clearly in his mind the heavy disgruntled face of Professor Hartley as he strode past the van with his weighty patriarchal tread. Alice, untying straps on the car, was as slight and as vulnerable as a peasant girl twisting ribbons around a maypole before the arrival of Cromwell in Michael's loving and historically flawed imagination. There was no chance that Alice, struggling with the blue tarpaulin, could have engaged in battle with the elephantine Professor. Michael waited for her, not as an expectant lover, but as a man faithfully performing the last rites. He waited because he said he would wait. He knew she would never come.

He filled in the time by telephoning his mother.

'Are you all right, dear?' she asked perceptively when he had said nothing but his initial 'hello' for long moments.

'Well, Aunty Sarah was dead,' Michael said with a sigh. 'And I was in love with this woman and we were going to use the house for an alternative therapy centre. But now I think her husband has got her, so I suppose she won't be allowed.'

'Oh dear,' Michael's mother said comfortingly. 'That's a pity, darling. What a shame. Did you say Sarah was dead?'

'Yes,' Michael said. 'Eventually.'

'Oh dear,' his mother said again. 'Never mind, dear. Are you eating enough?'

'Yes,' Michael said sadly.

'And who does your washing?'

'Laun-der-rette,' Michael sighed.

'Your father wants a word . . .' his mother said.

Michael looked up and out of the phone box.

The long silver-grey Jaguar car whispered around the corner and drew up beside the phone box. Alice leaned over and swung open the door.

'Gosh,' Michael said breathlessly.

'What's this I've been hearing?' the phone trumpeted. 'What's this about Sarah and some crackpot scheme of yours? If I have to come down to Suffix again you'll be sorry, young man! All of Sarah's estate is to be held in trust, Michael. Don't you go meddling with it. I'll get my man on to it first thing next week. Everything else can be dealt with by the doctor there, he's a solid sort of chap. Don't you go butting in when you're not wanted. You should be concentrating on your studies . . . I don't pay good money for you to . . .'

Michael, dazed, still holding the telephone, wandered towards the car, the curly telephone cable straightening and elongating behind him.

'Another thing,' the phone said nastily. 'I've been reading up on the statistics of graduate unemployment so there's no need for you to think you've got a meal-ticket for life . . .'

Alice, like Boadicea in her chariot, beamed at Michael. The reassuring smell of old leather and deeply polished teak enveloped him as his knees buckled beneath him and tipped him into the passenger seat of Professor Hartley's Jaguar.

'How?' he gulped.

Alice leaned across him and drew the door shut. It closed with a smooth 'chunk' sound which spoke loudly to Michael of thousands of pounds worth of craftsmanship. The car moved forward pulling firmly and relentlessly on the phone cable while the phone, held limply and completely unconsciously in Michael's hand, continued to convey the unending crackle of anger. Michael watched behind them in silent surprise as the stalk of the phone booth bowed towards them, and then twanged upright as the cable finally snapped. The snarl of Michael's father's instructions stopped abruptly. Michael absent-mindedly dropped the silent phone to the floor of the car.

'How?' he asked again.

Alice glanced at him swiftly, with her strong sweet smile and the car powered forward with its engine going 'purrahh purrahh, purrahh' especially softly. Michael felt his knees go all soppy.

'I bundled him,' she said simply.

'Unnhnnh?'

'I bundled him,' she repeated.

She glanced at Michael as she paused for a break in the traffic to let them out on to the main road.

Michael's reeling brain staggered in diminishing concentric circles inside the echoing caverns of his head. He knew that 'bundling' was a courtship ritual, much beloved of peasant folk in cold climates, whereby the affianced couple cuddle together under blankets and indulge in heavy petting. But she had only been gone seven minutes! And it was broad daylight! And Professor Hartley surely would not . . .?

'I threw the tarpaulin over his head,' she said.

The car moved forward and then leaped with a muted growl as Mrs Hartley hit the accelerator with a potent toe. 'It has elasticated straps,' she said contentedly. 'It was easy to roll him up, and easy to clip them on.'

She flicked Professor Hartley's right-hand indicator with contemptuous skill, and Professor Hartley's car moved out into the fast lane. The loudest noise was the elegant 'wink wink wink' of the little light bulb at the end of the indicator arm.

'You've left him?' Michael confirmed.

'Thrashing around like a netted elephant under the tarpaulin,' she said contentedly. 'It'll be hours before anyone gets him out.'

'Golly,' Michael said, inadequately.

Alice smiled. 'He gets claustrophobia,' she said. Her voice was silky with pleasure. 'He gets claustrophobia something rotten,' she said.

They did not go straight home. The afternoon sun was too tempting, the fine spring weather was urging birds to sing and lovers to play truant from work and duty. In the little pubs that fringe the South Downs, pallid area managers inveigled secretaries out for lunch and slid vodka into their grapefruit juices. Dozing reps forgot to phone their wives to tell them they would be late home for dinner. Commercial salesmen rested their suitcases of samples on those brass rails which ring traditional bars, for no reason known to man, unless they are there to cling to when drink has brought the customer so low that even lying prone on the floor will not keep it steady.

Alice and Michael, warmed by their illicit love and now by joint theft, as well as murder, fraud, deception and vandalism of a BT public phone box, cruised gaily around the South Downs lanes. Alice wound down the windows and the sweet light smell of the summer flowers flowed in like elderflower champagne. The sides of the grey Jaguar brushed against gypsy lace, bee orchids, scabious, and poppies in the hedgerows and collected sticky raindrops of nectar and a dusting of pale pollen. A small chalk blue butterfly, almost extinct as a species, but clinging on in favourable nooks and crannies of habitat, fluttered through the car, past Michael's ecstatically sniffing nose. It waggled its antennae at him, a friendly signal from one imperilled specimen to another.

Alice stopped the car in a gateway and they joined hands and walked together up the smooth turf slope to the crest of the hill. Small, star-like flowers grew

71

in the grass around Alice's feet, birds of one sort or another warbled and cheeped in a medley of sound attractive only to another bird of that specific sort or another. When they rested at the brow of the hill the whole of southern England seemed laid at their feet. Another bit of Sussex ahead of them, and a bit of something which was probably Kent to their right.

'Heaven,' Alice said contentedly. She lay back on the grass and lifted her face to the warm sunshine. A fat furry bee bumbled past them, drunk with cowslip pollen. High up in the blue sky a bird as small as a dot circled looking down, possibly an eagle, probably not.

'Breathe deeply,' Alice commanded. 'Be At One with Nature.'

And Michael, high on fear, drunk with success, hallucinating from lack of sleep and drained of every scrap of essence in him, breathed deeply, and deeply fell asleep.

They lay for an hour or two in the sunshine, like little babes in the woods, but when the sun went in and no kindly robins covered them with leaves Michael shivered and sat up.

'Cold!' he said to the empty hills.

Alice lazily opened her eyes and chuckled. 'Me too,' she said and sighed. 'I've not slept in the open air for years,' she said wonderingly. 'I'd forgotten how it felt.'

Michael leaped to his feet, alive with energy and joy. 'Race you to the car!' he yelled.

72

Alice sprang to her feet laughing. Scarves streaming behind her, she pursued him down the hill, her sandalled feet twinkling quickly over the grass. She ran well and they were neck and neck when they reached the car and laughing and breathless as they tumbled in.

Michael stretched in the comfort of the upholstered leather bucket seat as if he had driven in such a car every day of his life.

'This is nice,' he said, forgetting for a moment where it had come from. 'I've always wanted a car like this.'

'So have I,' said Alice, who had had a car like this in the garage of the house where she lived for the past sixteen years but never called it her own.

She drove carefully home, and when they reached the drive Michael got out and opened the gates, and then walked down the drive to open the garage doors for the car.

'Should we clean it?' he offered unwillingly, looking at the gleaming chrome now faintly dulled with dust and spotted with the excrement and corpses of very small flying creatures who had tested to their utmost Newton's Law of Motion and whose final thought was that the Law stinks.

'Oh no,' Alice said casually. 'We're not going to wash it, and polish it all the time. Personkind should not be enslaved by machines. We're free spirits, you and me, Michael.'

'Oh good,' Michael said. He fitted the door key into the lock and held out his hand to Alice. With a limpid smile she stepped inside the circle of his arm. Michael caressed her shoulder with newly assumed confidence and rising desire as they went inside. For the first time in their relationship Michael was about to make a sexual move which was not premature ejaculation.

'Alice,' he said seductively. 'Shall we . . .'

SUDDENLY THERE WAS A DREADFUL HAMMERING NOISE ON THE CEILING!

The blood drained from Michael's face; he was as sallow as Caerphilly cheese.

'What's that?' he hissed, glaring at Alice.

She was pale too, but she gathered up her long skirts and petticoats and scurried up the stairs, past the master bedroom where Aunty had been freed from her negative life force, across the landing to the spare bedroom where Aunty's corpse had been stored awaiting burial. The door was closed. From behind it came the peremptory, familiar knocking, and a cracked old voice yelling:

'Where's my sherry? It's past five o'clock. It's time for my sherry. Where is it?'

Alice's eyes darkened, and her jaw firmed. She threw open the door and the thumping abruptly stopped.

'Aunty Sarah, you should be dead!' she said crossly.

There was a split second of silence. Michael trembled in the void.

'I know!' the old voice cackled. 'They all say that!

74

The doctor! The daily! M'lawyer! They all say it, but I'll outlive them all! I'll outlive all of you! You too, Heidi, or whatever your name is! Now get me my sherry. And I'll have chicken in tarragon again tonight. It's my favourite. And that cheesecake pudding with chocolate ice-cream. I need building up after the sleep I had this afternoon. I can't remember when I slept so well. Scurry about, Heidi! It's *Top of the Pops* on the radiovision later!'

Alice shut the door so softly that it scarcely clicked. She walked downstairs with her graceful measured tread. She went past Michael and her face was blank. He followed her, like an imprinted duckling, into the kitchen and watched her sink on to the kitchen chair and rest her head in her hands.

Nobody spoke for quite a long time.

'I find I don't quite like your Aunty Sarah,' Alice said after a little while.

Michael breathed out with a gasp which sounded like a squeak of assent.

'She has a remarkably strong Life Force,' Alice conceded. 'But I don't find her . . . sympathetic!'

'No,' Michael agreed.

Alice sighed, as many women sigh who have the care of elderly relatives thrust upon them and little help (Lord knows) from the Social Services; and don't mention the Voluntary because it's just more old ladies only a little more skittish.

'Michael, I shall have to give you a shopping list,' she said wearily. 'You'll have to go into the town, you can take the Jaguar. She wants chicken in tarragon for dinner and I don't have any meat in my freezer. I'll write down what I need.'

Michael nodded sorrowfully. His passing idea of snatching Alice on the threshold of their new home had fled as soon as he heard the hammering. He could scarcely remember what it felt like to feel his manhood coursing through his loins or anywhere else, come to that.

'All right,' he said humbly.

Alice drew a pad and a pen towards her and wrote out Michael's shopping list for Aunty's supper. Michael took it and then paused. This is what it said:

3 pieces of fresh chicken
1 packet dried tarragon
1 carton single cream
1 live black cockerel
10 cloves garlic
1 new (wrapped) meat cleaver with wood handle
1 box white chalk
1 box rock salt
1 bottle witch hazel
1 rock crystal
1 white nightgown
20 wax white candles
1 antique sword or dagger

'I don't have enough money for all this,' he said, glancing down the ingredients.

Alice sighed patiently, went to her rucksack and drew out Professor Hartley's housekeeping money. 'Use this,' she said. 'It should be enough.'

Michael nodded, he stepped towards Alice and kissed her lightly on the cheek.

'Don't be upset,' he said nobly. 'You have no cause for regrets. I will release you. It's all right with me if you want to leave. You can always go home.'

A mournful smile flickered across Alice's pale face as she thought of her home stripped of belongings, and her husband enmeshed and bound in his blue plastic car-cover thrashing around the university car park, the stolen furniture, the kidnapped car, the insulted marital counsellor.

'Yes,' she said. 'I suppose I can.'

Michael nodded, pleased that he had found the right thing to say – something to cheer her up. 'Won't be long,' he said sweetly, and went.

Alice sat for a long while in the sunny kitchen on her own. There was a frenzied knocking upstairs from time to time but Alice ignored it. She glanced at Michael's jacket, left carelessly over the back of one of the kitchen chairs. The black cover of a diary showed, poking out of a pocket. Without hesitation Alice took it out and opened it. She turned to January the First; there was the usual January the First entry.

Got this from Mummy. Really mean to keep a diary all year. Can look back on it for memoirs. Should be really interesting – back to university, mixing with people who will run the country in the future etc. Shall make an entry every day. Starting today.

77

So here goes!

January 1st *Nothing much happened.*

January 2nd *Really plan to keep this up. Second day Second entry! So far so good. Nothing much happened.*

January 3rd *Nothing much happened. Wish I was back at Suffix. Nothing ever happens here.*

January 4th *Mummy made me go to church with her. It was really boring. Nothing happened.*

January 5th *Nothing at all happened today.*

There then followed a flutter of blank pages. Alice idly turned to the back of the book and her attention sharpened.

People I wish I knew, and their phone numbers
1. Sarah Underwood is the president of the Lesbian Actresses Association. I wish I were a girl and then she would fancy me. Her phone is 63241.
2. John Cleary – (80688) they say he deals in drugs!!!!
3. Ruth Maxwell (97364) but she is gay too.
4. Stephen Simmonds – anyway I know him. He says he and Ruth Maxwell did it, but I know he did not. (97867)

Alice scanned the list. Without conscious intent Michael had listed the sexual preferences of the

natural leaders of his year – some fifty names. And
he had listed their phone numbers too. Alice, with
her mind on the arrival of her friends that evening,
and her heart yearning towards an alternative
therapy centre despite the yells of protest from the
upstairs bedroom, scanned the list with a growing
smile. Then she took the diary and, reading it as she
walked, went back to the sitting-room and started
telephoning again.

Michael was as quick as he could be, but there
were a number of small purchases on his list not
stocked by the supermarket. The live black cockerel
was a particular problem until he remembered a pet
shop on the outside of town. He also had some
trouble in parking the car since he could not find
reverse gear and the gear lever was too refined to
engrave vulgar instructions on the knob at the top.
It took him a little forethought to go to an out-of-
town hypermarket where the car park was suf-
ficiently empty for him to drive forwards to park,
and forwards to the exit.

Thereafter he parked outside shops and drove
away again, all in the same direction. It naturally
took him a little longer to get home since if a car
parked in front of him Michael had to wait for it to
move away before he could escape; but he enjoyed
the practice, and the car – which until today had
never before gone further than the university and
back – perhaps enjoyed the journey.

It was half past eight before Michael paused outside the gates of Rithering Manor, judging them for

distance, and then got out and paced the curve, before cruising carefully up the drive. He was not a confident driver and the curve of the drive was awkward, so that it was a quarter to nine before he parked the car in the driveway and went in by the front door. It was only then that he noticed that there were a lot of other cars in the driveway, and the house was brightly lit. There was music playing loudly, and the high joyful sound of older women laughing without their husbands in earshot. Michael stumbled in, his arms full of groceries, and then reeled to a standstill.

It was a party.

It was a tremendous party.

And Aunty Sarah was there, still in her white nightgown and white cap but with a brilliant rainbow shawl thrown over her shoulders which Michael recognized as one of Alice's. Most of the Suffix Theatre Players were there, Michael recognized the Lesbian Actress-tors Association, who insisted on playing cross-dressing parts, generally Shakespeare; and their hapless young male hangers-on who weakly agreed at casting meetings to wear dresses if the women thought that was the real message of the play. There were a whole load of older women whom Michael had never seen before, but one or two seemed vaguely familiar. Surely that woman sprawled along the back of the chair, her hand possessively clenched on the belt of Peter Travis, was the Vice-chancellor's wife? And the grey-haired woman lying on the floor, dipping grapes into wine and feeding them to Michael's friend Stephen, was the Dean's sister?

Michael blinked. If this was not a particularly feverish nightmare (as he had first most reasonably supposed) then there was a party going on, in Aunty Sarah's house, with Aunty Sarah entertaining all of the senior faculty wives and most of Michael's young male or lesbian friends.

Michael dropped the bag of groceries, and at the noise Alice glanced around and came over to greet him, stepping casually around a woman who looked not unlike the university chaplain's wife, who seemed to be nuzzling the neck of one of the university's Gay Rights activists (Women's Section).

'Darling,' she said delightedly. 'Welcome to the inaugural party of the SAM – Sarah, Alice and Michael – Growth Centre! Isn't it a wonderful surprise?'

'Mmmminnnnnhhhh?' Michael demanded.

'I knew you'd be thrilled,' Alice cried, linking her arm in his. 'And look at Sarah,' she said.

'Sssaaammmnnn?' Michael almost queried.

'It worked better than I could have dreamed!' Alice said. 'Of course she was angry and unsympathetic. She's been cooped up in that poxy little room ever since the end of the war.'

'Waaahhhrrr?' Michael interrogated.

'Yes!' Alice exclaimed. 'I don't even know which war! She could have been there for years!' She glanced over at Aunty Sarah who was sucking with a peaceful expression on an enormous curved meerschaum pipe. 'Extreme sexual dysfunction,' Alice said in an undertone. 'Coupled with raging hypochondria, an excessive power drive, over-capitalized and under-used.'

Michael ceased his contributions to Alice's discussion and instead lifted his head and sniffed. He was not part of the élite of Suffix who habitually smoked cannabis, but none the less he had sat and breathed behind a few ageing postgrads at lectures on existentialism, and he recognized the smell of the smoke which was hanging heavy in the air of Aunty Sarah's sitting-room, weaving its attractive, irresistible web from Aunty Sarah's pipe; which, even as he yelped in horror, made him giggle and watch, sniggering, as Aunty Sarah got high, high, high as a housemartin. And all around her the Faculty Wives Support Group ate magic mushroom canapés, and cannabis-and-chocolate brownies, and hung loose with inadequate and sexually over-anxious kids, young enough to be their children.

'And so delicious,' said the wife of the Dean as she pitched her face down into the expectant lap of Michael's friend George who had, until this evening, worn a Marilyn Monroe wig and insisted on being called Georgie.

Michael felt his world perceptions roll and creak and shift.

Alice pressed a hand-rolled cigarette into his limp fingers.

'I don't . . .' he stammered. 'I promised my father I'd never . . .'

82

She laughed indulgently. 'Silly boy,' she said, her dark eyes warm with love. 'This isn't anything bad. It's herbal tobacco. It's all organic!'

It was only later that night, after everyone, including Aunty Sarah, had taken their clothes off and danced about the flowery garden in the white un-judging moonlight, and then collapsed in a heap of communal affection and exhausted sexuality, did Michael remember to ask Alice which herb when smoked in enormous quantities makes people take their clothes off and giggle about their husbands.

And it was at dawn that Alice, rearranging the rainbow shawl around Aunty Sarah's naked shoulders as the old lady lay in a fretwork of slim young limbs, said dozily, 'Cannabis leaf, darling. Very useful for constipation. That's why I gave so much to Aunty Sarah.'

And Michael, his head pillowed on the warm breasts of the Dean's wife, and the limp Blinkie softly held by Alice, nodded sleepily and said plaintively: 'I get constipated too, you know.'

Alice smiled at him under her long dark eyelashes. 'We all do,' she said profoundly.

FRIDAY

The morning, when they all awoke – the two dozen or so of them, casually coupled in strange tangles like a new and alternative Rubik cube puzzle, sorting out first: whose bodies belonged to whom, and then: who owned which sandals and scarves and 501 jeans – the morning could have been embarrassing. But Alice made it seem the continuation of a delightful party. Not a hangover, not an end of something, but a wonderful and promising start.

'Now!' she said importantly when everyone had drifted through to the kitchen and was eating damp and doughy wholemeal bread and drinking herbal tea. 'Now! I have prepared some lifestyle analyses and some personal programmes which I want to talk through with each of you in detail. I shall be in the dining-room and I will see each one of you for an individual consultation. Michael will show you in.'

She swept past them all, through the connecting door into the dining-room. Michael could hear her singing softly as she whisked the dust sheets off the imposing mahogany dining-table. He scurried in after her.

'What d'you want me to do?' he demanded.

Alice turned and smiled at him.

'Send them in, one at a time,' she said. 'When I've seen each one, send them out of the front door. Take at least twenty pounds off each of them, that's the enrolment fee. They'll pay more when they're really growing.'

Alice met Michael's blank look of utter ungrowing incomprehension and shrugged her firm white shoulders under her white peasant blouse. Her dark red skirt swished as she moved purposefully about the room.

'Mi – chael,' she said silkily.

Michael guppled (initially a typing error, but so perfect a description of his action I cannot bring myself to conform with the limited vocabulary of people who discount such insights).

'Yes?' he said.

'Out there,' she said, nodding her head to the kitchen door. 'There are more than a dozen women who have had nothing like a satisfactory sexual experience for years. For years, Michael!'

Michael guppled again and nodded.

'Out there also are a number of young people who are urgently seeking sexual experience with partners of any age, race, persuasion, or gender and failing signally to find anyone.'

Michael nodded again. His lonely evenings in his

room, and his fevered fantasies into his abused foam-rubber pillow were too recent to be denied.

Alice smiled confidently. 'We bring them together,' she said. 'They grow.'

There was something troubling Michael in the back of his mind, but he was not sure how he could phrase it without giving offence to Alice.

'Is this *really* what a growth centre does, darling?' he asked.

Alice smiled. 'You work in the ways which come to hand,' she said certainly. 'Look at Sarah! I brought her back to life when conventional doctors had pronounced her dead, didn't I?'

Michael nodded. Sort of.

'Look at Mary Daley, the university chaplain's wife! All that anxiety about the spiritual purity of their marriage and it turns out that she really prefers girls!'

Michael nodded. Possibly.

'Look at us!' Alice breathed. 'Aren't we the best, the very best thing which has ever happened to either of us?'

Michael melted, utterly convinced. Yes, oh yes, oh yes. Blinkie The Phallus, weary from the exertions of last night, none the less stirred feebly, and reminded of last night, yearned once more.

'Well then!' Alice said triumphantly. And when Michael did not respond other than to make a little moaning noise of lust she nodded at him. 'This is the way forward!' she said. 'It is a perfect and traditional partnership. The older woman and the younger man. The older woman and the younger woman.

'There is no reason', she added, her voice hardening slightly, 'why mature, not to say elderly, not to say disgusting old men should be the only ones who seek and find young partners.'

'Right,' Michael said, as if he understood anything. 'So I show them in to you, one at a time. Right!'

It worked rather well actually.

To Michael's young friends Mrs Hartley had the authority of a seer. They had all suffered well-fed childhoods and excessively good educations so they were naturally faddish in their eating habits and averse to complex ideas and the process of logical reasoning. For them, Mrs Hartley's spiritual certainties, her understanding and tolerance of their sexual inadequacies and her disdain for their academic studies all indicated a leader they would pay good money to follow.

For Mrs Hartley's friends, the faculty wives, any medical or spiritual system which permitted or even acknowledged female lust would have been a merciful relief. For years they had repressed their sexual desires in good works, miserably cruel exercise programmes, or half-baked Eastern philosophies. For years they had ignored or discounted their sexual frustration – accusing their nerves, their allergies, their menstrual problems – anything but acknowledge the fact that they had seriously hot pants and no prospect of relief. Mrs Hartley's joyous call to get in touch with Nature, with the ebb and thrust of natural energy as exemplified in young male students, and her detailed description of the rising of the essences of young partners, called to their deepest souls, to their hearts and to other nearby and more demanding organs.

Then Mrs Hartley wrote them out strict detoxification programmes in which they had to give up all their favourite foods and drinks, and then she stung them for a week's housekeeping money. They left with a feeling of being richly rolled over, in every sense of the word.

And they all made appointments to return.

Sarah and Alice were sitting either side of the kitchen table when Michael came back into the kitchen, after waving off the last newly enrolled client, swinging a tea towel held at the corners like a sack stuffed with coins and paper money; and from the faculty wives substantial cheques drawn on joint accounts with lies on the cheque stubs ready for their husbands' inspection.

'How did we do?' Alice demanded.

'We've got nearly six hundred pounds here,' Michael said, awe-struck. 'I've never even seen so much cash!'

Alice smiled. 'More tea, Sarah?' she asked casually, and poured her another cup.

Michael looked nervously at his elderly relation. She was wearing this morning an ancient purple dress which reached to the floor, heavily encrusted with jet beads. A black toque hat with purple egret feathers nodded on her head.

'Oughtn't you be resting in bed?' he asked. He was ransacking his brain trying to remember the night before. Aunty Sarah surely had been with them when they were dancing in the moonlight. But it was not possible, it could not be remotely possible, that she had been there when everyone had come back into the house, stretched out before the fire and rummaged in each other's warm bodies for their own private satisfactions. That could not have taken place.

Aunty Sarah beamed at him, the discontented old wrinkles around her eyes crazing like a good-tempered alligator.

'I should think I ought,' she said. 'I'm shagged out.'

Alice smiled understandingly. 'You pop up to bed then, darling,' she said easily. 'Have a nice rest. I'll call you in plenty of time for lunch. You're doing your oral history class this afternoon remember.'

Alice nodded to Michael and explained: 'Sarah is leading a group exploring the oppression of women throughout the ages, by reaching deep into our own histories. It should be fascinating.'

Michael nodded with convulsive and meaningless movements like one of those dogs which used to be popular seated in the back windows of cars to irritate other drivers.

'She has some especially interesting things to say about the young men of the Great War,' Alice said. 'Some really interesting revelations about the lost generation.'

'Wankers,' the old lady said in her clear upper-class voice. 'And poufs, most of them.'

Michael's blank bemused gaze nodded around towards his elderly relative.

'I thought you were bedridden,' he said wonderingly. 'I thought you couldn't walk.'

'Nowhere to go,' she said, as if that were sufficient explanation. As Michael still looked blank she laughed, setting the purple egret feathers jiggling. 'Nowhere to go, nothing to do,' she said.

'Sarah took to her bed after a shock,' Alice explained. 'She never got up again and after a while people simply assumed she could not walk.'

'Betty Foster's tea dance,' the old lady said with sudden energy as the memory came vividly back. 'There she was, proud as punch in pillar-box red silk. And my Ma making me wear nothing but bloody white all the time.'

Alice nodded, her face as sweet and understanding as a priest hearing confession.

'Pissed me off,' the old lady said. 'No decent men around anyway, and Vaughan Sutcliffe trailing about after her all afternoon, teaching her to Charleston for God's sake. Came home in a temper, kissed the chauffeur for spite, caught by Pa in the back seat of the Rolls with my knickers down. Nothing else I could do.'

Michael gawped helplessly and gazed at Alice for translation.

'Fainted,' the old lady said. A cunning smile came into her eyes. 'Chauffeur was a clever lad,' she said reminiscently. 'Told my Pa he was resuscitating me. Funny way to go about it I'd have thought.'

'Did your father believe him?' Alice asked, smiling.

'Had to!' Sarah said. 'Most men would believe anything rather than think that women are normal human beings. Besides,' she said consideringly, 'brains don't run on the male side in my family. You might have noticed with young Michael here.'

Alice did not deny this, Michael noted.

'Took to my bed,' she recounted. 'Carried down to the parlour every day by the chauffeur, carried upstairs again every night. Convenient that. Had my few flings. But never met a man worth getting up for.'

'I thought you were ill,' Michael said.

Aunty Sarah smiled gently at him. Her old face gleamed with hard-won wisdom and an aged toughness.

'Lots of ways of getting your own way,' she said. 'But if you're a gel, it's best to be sneaky.'

She gave a little yawn.

'You'd better have your rest,' Alice said gently.

Aunty Sarah got up from the kitchen table and waited before the kitchen door until Michael jumped up to open it for her.

She paused as she went past him and Michael froze, wondering what was coming next. She patted his cheek with a hand half-encased in a violet lace mitten. 'You'd be worth getting up for,' she said proudly. 'Take after me, you do! Proper little alley-cat you are! I enjoyed watching you.'

She smiled her sweet little-old-lady smile at him and

went upstairs. They heard her steady step up to the spare bedroom, and the closing of her bedroom door.

There was a short silence.

'Does she know about Thomas the cat?' Michael asked irrelevantly.

Alice glanced at him. 'She's forgotten all about him,' she said. 'She is nearly ninety you know, Michael. You must make some allowances.'

'Are we allowed to stay here?' he asked. 'Even though . . .' he tailed off.

'Even though I cured her and she's still alive?' Alice asked. 'Oh yes.'

'So . . .' Michael's little voice shrank away to nothing.

Alice waited.

'So what do we do now then?' he asked feebly.

Alice rose from the table and stretched languorously. Her large breasts pressed against the thin translucent cotton of her peasant blouse, visibly contradicting theories about the idiocy of rural life. Any class which can design clothes of such moral hypocrisy that they manage to be tremulously innocent and irresistibly arousing at the same time needs little advice from *fin-de-siècle*, anally obsessed, German intellectuals.

'I think . . .' she said sweetly, 'that we should follow Aunty's example and have a little nap. She's teaching oral history this afternoon, I'm doing lunar cycles and female arousal, and you' – she glanced at a sheaf of notes – 'you are taking Mrs Wheatley on a one-to-one counselling session.'

'I am?' Michael gaped. 'Which one is Mrs Wheatley?'

Alice slid past the table and swayed towards the door. 'She's the one with the nervous stammer,' she said. 'Her husband is Doctor Wheatley, the famous art historian who specializes in classical art and the male nude.' Alice nodded wisely. 'There is no doubt in *my* mind about Doctor Wheatley's preferences,' she said.

'Oh, that one!' Michael said, relieved to understand something at last. 'But what do I do with his wife?'

Alice paused beside him, twined her strong white arms around his neck and looked deeply into his red-rimmed eyes. 'Anything she can afford,' she said softly, and melted into his kiss.

It was good that the house was big and soundly built. Aunty Sarah's class took place in the sitting-room at the front of the house and you could hear the screams of malicious laughter from the kitchen, even with both doors shut. Alice's session on lunar cycles and female arousal was more scientific – Alice used Professor Hartley's flip chart to good effect and with joyful disregard of the price of paper. From time to time she ordered the curtains drawn so that she could use his overhead projector. She had eyed these artefacts for decades of inferiority and she took especial pleasure in drawing pictures of female genitalia with Professor Hartley's special overhead projector felt-tip pens, which, for sixteen years, she had been expressly forbidden to touch.

'I feel deeply released,' she breathed at Michael as they passed in the hall.

Michael felt deeply released too. He had been a little nervous of Mrs Wheatley. Alice's instructions had been ambiguous and she had done nothing more to help him than give him a little snack of bright scarlet mushrooms on toast and light a fire for him in the dining-room.

'Just do what she wants and charge her thirty pounds,' she said.

When Michael blinked she had smiled. 'People don't value things they get for free,' she said. For a moment Michael had a vision of years and years of dinners and washing-up and Alice's hopeful face handing out plates and receiving back garbage.

'The more she pays for it, the more good it does her,' she said wisely.

Then the doorbell had rung and Mrs Wheatley had hovered nervously on the tiled hall floor.

'It's me,' she said, as if she were reluctant to force her name on Michael, this early in their acquaintanceship.

'Hullo,' Michael said. 'What would you like to do?'

Alice spread her arms wide and shooed them into the dining-room, leaving them alone, closing the door behind them. As she paused in the hall for one second she could hear Mrs Wheatley's voice quaver, crack and then wail through tears:

'Oh, Michael! Since I was seventeen no one has ever . . . no man has ever . . . I've never dared ask anyone to do . . . YOU KNOW WHAT!'

Alice smiled and went away from the door.

From time to time during the afternoon she hovered in the hall to listen. Most of the time she could hear nothing but breathless little sighs. Once Mrs Wheatley said clearly: 'I saw a book once with a picture in it, and the man was kind of turned, so that this bit was up against there like this . . .'

And Michael replied rather breathlessly, 'What, like this?'

Mrs Wheatley's hushed giggle was somehow smothered. 'I think I must have seen the book upside down,' she said.

Then there was silence again for a while.

All the classes broke up at about four. Aunty Sarah, spry and beaming, had made them a big pot of tea and Alice took a large carrot cake from the deep freeze, microwaved it to near-edibility, and cut everyone substantial slices.

Michael ate like a ravenous wolf. Alice and Mrs Wheatley watched him with misty fondness. For one moment their eyes met and Mrs Wheatley smiled at Alice, and blushed like a girl.

After tea, a couple of the lunar cycles group and three of Aunty Sarah's oral history group offered to make supper for the rest. Alice waved them towards the freezer as she drifted out to the garden to sit under the apple trees where the apple blossom snowed down on the grass and bees reeled pie-eyed, or perhaps pie-antennaed, on cider-like pollen.

'Mrs Hartley?'

Alice opened her eyes. Before her was one of her students from the lunar cycles and female arousal course, an intense, dark girl, one of Michael's set from the drama centre. In Alice's afternoon seminar it had become clear that this girl had enjoyed neither arousal nor a lunar cycle, having managed to resist womanhood and even adolescence by the simple but effective technique of giving up food. She was painfully thin. At her neck one could see the little bird-bones of her pipe-cleaner skeleton. Her legs were so thin one might, absent-mindedly, tie a message to them if the telephone was out of order. It was her bad luck that just when the madness of her family had prompted her to resist adulthood the madness of the fashion scene had decreed that this half-starved asexual shape was the ideal. Therefore Stephanie, and all the girls like her, denied their bodies' hunger, swathed themselves in layers of grey and black cloth reminiscent of shrouds, and had the satisfaction of knowing themselves to be at the very pinnacle of the woman-hating, sexuality-fearing fashion machine.

Alice, resplendent in deep red skirt, white blouse, orange headscarf and purple shawl with tinkling bells around her shoulders, shaded her dark eyes with her broad white hand and smiled up.

'Yes, Stephanie?'

'Mrs Hartley, we'd like to dance!' Stephanie said

in a little rush of breathy whisper. 'We're missing our aerobics class in town, and we thought, if you didn't mind, we could do it here.'

Alice waved a generous arm at the house. 'Of course,' she said sweetly. 'Do you know enough to lead the class?'

A dull red sneaked up through Stephanie's tiny arteries.

'I think so,' she said.

'Two pounds each,' Alice said beneficently. 'Come and see me when you've finished.'

Stephanie danced off, her tiny feet hardly bending the grass blades of the orchard, and left Alice in sun-drenched solitude. Birds tweeped approvingly in the trees above her head. In the distance Alice could hear the rumble of someone's motor mower. At One with Nature, Alice let the grass grow under her and all around her. She closed her eyes and gave herself up for sleep.

She dozed for only a few moments before curiosity got the better of her. Faintly from the house she could hear the deep thud of a bass guitar and the insistent beat of drums keeping time for the patter of light feet as they jogged and jumped in obedience to Stephanie's squeaked commands. Alice got to her feet and strolled through the sap-springing orchard, through the derelict garden, up to the house.

Michael, asleep for the second time that day in Professor Hartley's big double bed, stirred uneasily and rolled on to his back. The thump of the music entered into his dreams and prompted visions of large-bodied older women with crows'-feet around their eyes, and sad, downturned mouths. Michael floated in his sleep, bursting with potency, full of essence, able to heal, restore, renovate. He felt like an organic source of T-Cut. He felt like a god. And all this power and strength came from doing what he had wanted to do more than anything else in the world ever since he was thirteen. Michael snored deeply.

Alice, peeping through the door, smiled and left him sleeping. She was drawn downstairs to the source of the music in the dining-room. She did not want to disturb the dancers so she went quietly into the kitchen, opened the serving hatch a crack, and peeped in.

Half a dozen girls had cleared the room for action. The warm Persian rugs were rolled up and stacked against the wall. The dining-room table was pushed back and the chairs carefully placed on top of it.

In the middle of the room, Stephanie was prancing like an animated Lowry picture, a pin-person in motion. Before her, five other women were echoing her gestures, like large blobby shadows behind a tiny twig.

Alice watched them. Two of them were young friends of Stephanie, both slight, one a little plumper than the other. The plumper one had beads of sweat on her upper lip and she stamped her feet with especial emphasis and eyed Stephanie's boney thinness with a look of utter envy.

The rest of the women were younger than Alice, but older than Stephanie. One or two were young faculty wives, their tummies round, their hips thickened. They danced watching the clock, they would have to collect children from child-minders or from school. One or two were postgraduate students, spreading at the hips from years of seated work.

Two thousand years of progress had brought these women to this pitch of leisure and education. None of them had ever hauled on a rope, none of them had ever heaved wet sheets through a wringer. None of them had ever stooped and lifted and carried weights heavier than a plastic carrier-bag full of shopping. As Alice watched, musing, she saw them dance through exercises which mimicked hauling on ropes, lifting wet sheets, heaving and carrying loads.

'Funny,' she thought.

The music changed abruptly.

'Now we'll work on our bums,' Stephanie said brightly. The whole group collapsed to the floor in a disciplined heap and lay panting noisily on their backs. As Alice watched, her eyes widening in surprise, they heaved their pelvises towards the ceiling and swung their hips first to the right, and then to the left and then thrust straight up and down in movements which could only be described as convulsive.

'Push!' Stephanie shrieked encouragingly. 'Clench those buttocks! Push . . . and . . . push . . . and push . . . and push!'

Upstairs in his sleep, Michael's smile broadened.

Downstairs, Alice swung the hatch wider and watched openly.

These women, she thought, were not getting enough basic exercise during the day. Nor were they getting enough basic exercise at night.

The Growth Centre could help people who wanted to push with their pelvises. The Growth Centre could use people who wanted to lift heavy weights and pull things.

Alice's mind ranged over the derelict orchard and the deep-rooted weeds. The large trunks of old rotting trees which overhung the drive, the fencing which was holed and patchy, the pot-holed drive which needed a fresh load of gravel fetching and spreading.

She nodded wisely, and smiled at Stephanie who was showing the class how to lie flat on your back, raise your legs vertically in the air and then bob up and try to knock yourself out by smashing your face on your knees. Alice shut the hatch and went to the sitting-room and drew some notepaper towards her.

'"Gardening Therapy Course,"' she wrote. '"NB see Voltaire's *Candide*."'

Eleven of them sat down to supper. Aunty Sarah stayed resting in her room but came down when there was no danger of having to do the washing-up. A couple of Michael's friends from university dropped in and talked about veganism and the peace movement. They, three of the younger women, and Stephanie, asked to stay the night and Alice raided the linen cupboard and found enough sheets, blankets and pillows for all of them.

They all went to bed early. The moon was in an interesting stage of the cycle and Alice wanted to lie with moonlight on her face. She stirred but did not waken at the continual patter of bare feet crossing and re-crossing the landing during the night. In the morning everyone contributed ten pounds each to demonstrate commitment to the communal spirit of the Growth Centre.

'How are we doing?' Michael asked when the last guest had gone, and he and Alice were sitting alone at the scrubbed kitchen table.

Alice pulled the second tea towel full of money towards her.

'I think we're making something like three hundred pounds a day,' she said after a few minutes. 'That's gross, mind.'

'It *is* gross,' Michael agreed.

Alice started scribbling on paper for a few moments, then she lifted her head and said: 'If we can do the courses for which we already have students, and some other things come up, then I think the Growth Centre will make something like eighty thousand pounds clear profit in the first year.'

Michael blinked. 'My father will be terribly pleased,' he said. 'He didn't seem to be too keen on us living here. He'll be amazed when he knows we're making money.'

Alice shot a glance at him. 'You've spoken to your father?' she asked carefully, keeping her voice light.

Michael nodded. 'I always talk to them on a Thursday. Father takes the afternoon off from the office to play golf, so first I talk to Mother and then I talk to Father.'

Alice was uncomfortable but she kept her face serene and nodded. Professor Hartley would have been warned at once by that especial pleasant blankness; but Michael saw only polite interest. 'When did you do this?' she asked.

'While I was waiting for you at the drama centre,' Michael said easily. 'I suddenly remembered and went to the pay phone. I always reverse the charges anyway.'

Alice let out one minute fearful breath. 'And did you tell them all about us?' she asked.

'Oh yes!' Michael's smile was happy. 'They didn't say much, but then they never do. I told them that Aunty Sarah was dead after your herbal tea and that we were in love, except that I thought you'd have to go back to your husband. I didn't tell them about the Growth Centre because I didn't know then that it had started.'

Michael got up to put the kettle on. Alice waited for more horrors, but he seemed to have nothing further to add.

'And what did your mother say?' Alice asked, her voice determinedly under control.

'She asked who was doing my laundry,' Michael said matter-of-factly.

Alice's growing sense of panic was overtaken by bewilderment. 'Laundry?' she asked.

Michael hastened to reassure her. 'It's OK,' he said. 'I do it at the university launderette, on Saturday night.'

Alice blinked. 'You told her that Sarah was dead and that you were living with me except that I had gone back to my husband, and she asked you about your laundry?'

'She always asks about my laundry,' Michael said reasonably. He saw Alice was looking bemused. 'It's how she shows her love,' he said with dignity. 'She asks about my laundry and I tell her I have enough clean underwear. It's how we communicate affection in my family.'

Alice nodded. She had a sense of rapidly gathering doom, and the news that Michael's family were all as crazy as coots was not helping.

'And your father?' she asked. 'What did he say?'

Michael screwed up his eyes to aid the process of memory. 'Oh, the usual things I expect,' he said, absent-minded. '"When are you going to get some work done?" and "when I was your age I was half-way through my apprenticeship", and "if I have to come down and see that nancy personal tutor of yours again there'll be trouble", and "whatever you do, Michael, don't get tied up with drugs and women", and "don't come running to me when you run out of money because I haven't got any".'

'Did he say anything about Sarah? About me?' Alice asked.

'We got cut off,' Michael said. He frowned as he cast his mind back to the conversation. 'Oh yes!

That's how the phone got into the Jaguar. You ripped the phone out of the box when you drove off, Alice.'

Alice looked utterly blank. She had not noticed the phone in Michael's hand. 'But your father,' she pursued. 'Did he say he was going to do anything about Sarah? About this house?'

Michael looked vague. 'I think he said not to do anything, and not to touch anything,' he offered. 'He generally doesn't like anyone doing anything very much.'

Alice nodded. 'He doesn't sound as if he has a very positive Life Force,' she said absently.

Michael shook his head with anxious emphasis. 'No, no, Alice,' he said. 'He'll go on for ever. Besides, it's all tied up in insurance policies and trusts, and you wouldn't like their house.'

Alice hadn't quite meant that, but she saw little point in correcting Michael. She had a sensation of dread clutching in a familiar way around her gut. She had thought that the Growth Centre was safe with her abilities, Aunty Sarah's support and Michael's unstoppable essences. But now, like an Eve in a latter-day Eden, Alice learned fear.

'Where do they live?' she asked. She was hoping that Michael would say Arbroath or the Isle of Man.

'Tunbridge Wells,' he said cheerfully. 'Nice and close. They'll probably pop over and see us next week sometime. I said they should. In fact, now I think of it, Dad said he'd be down as soon as he could. And that he would get his man on to it. That'll be nice, won't it?' He smiled happily at Alice. 'They always like to meet my friends,' he said cheerily.

SATURDAY

The aerobic gardening class was a remarkable success. Stephanie had been hesitant about the concept, arguing wasps and stinging nettles; but when she saw the large hi-fi speakers loaned with unconscious generosity by the university drama centre, and heard the heavy drum beat echoing in the overgrown garden, she was inspired. Alice explained that all aerobic dance was substitute work, performed as an inadequate alternative to hard manual labour. Their bodies were, in fact, crying out for the drudgery of rural toil. Alice grew persuasively anthropological about the alienation of women from their natural work. She explained how women since the dawn of time have heaved things, lifted things, cleared and gardened. Alice urged them to be authentic, to get in touch with their inheritance, with Nature, to get to grips with reality, and offered them – instead of little dances with chopping motions of the hands – the real thing: axes and half a dozen fallen trees to work on.

Ten pupils had arrived for the aerobics class this

morning: a pair of identical and indistinguishable twins who introduced themselves shyly as Gary and Timofy, and their friend Jonafon, as well as two new faculty wives, who arrived lugging babies in backpacks and looking harassed.

'Leave them with me!' Alice cried. 'I love babies! And you must be exhausted. What you need is an hour's aerobo-work and then half an hour's relaxation.'

Two pairs of eyes shadowed black with exhaustion from sleepless nights and loneliness boggled helplessly at Alice.

'Poor darlings!' Alice said to them. 'Babies are a blessing, but such hard work.'

Tears welled up in the eyes of the shorter woman. She staggered slightly as Alice lifted the backpack off her. 'I wanted a pram,' she said sadly. 'But he said that it should be carried. They all say you've got to carry them these days.'

Alice popped the baby out of the backpack like a tight-fitting pea from a pod.

'Babies need the feeling of closeness,' said the other woman in a dulled monotone. 'They need to feel close to Mother, all day, all night, every day, every night.'

'Of course,' Alice said, matter-of-fact. 'Of course babies need the feeling of closeness. But *you* need the feeling of distance.'

The second woman gasped, it was as if Alice had sworn in a church.

'They need to hear Mother's heartbeat,' she said,

repeating the lesson. 'They need to feel Mother's movement.'

'Oh yes,' Alice agreed readily. 'They'd like that all the time. But they're born now, aren't they? Can't go on listening to your stomach gurgling all their lives. They'll have to get used to it sooner or later. *You* don't get exactly what you want all the time, do you?'

The two young women gazed at Alice with red-rimmed eyes. They looked like long-stay prisoners of the Bastille on the morning of July 14th. They looked like they had *never* got exactly what they wanted – at any time.

The taller one's lip quivered as she fought back tears. 'He won't ever lie in his cot!' she said despairingly. 'He'll only sleep if I walk him. And if I stop walking he wakes up and cries! Up and down on the landing, all night long. I must have walked to London and back half a dozen times. The only time he sleeps is when he hears David's key in the door. As soon as he hears the front door open and David shout, "I'm home, I've had a bloody awful day, pour me a drink for God's sake," he falls at once into deep sleep and makes darling little snores and David tells me I'm too tense! He tells me that it's *me* that's keeping him awake. Of course I'm tense!' she said, her voice a squeak of suppressed rage. 'I've not slept for months, I walk farther every night than I've ever walked before in my life, and when I complain David says, "Really, Suzanne, you wanted the baby, you know." As if I ever knew what I was getting myself into!'

Alice clucked comfortingly. 'Little horror,' she said with a loving smile. 'Tuck him in bed beside you, lovey, and drink a stiff gin before you feed him. It'll settle him down in no time.'

The shorter woman gulped. 'If you knew . . .' she started, her sobs drowning out her words. Alice, with the baby gurgling wetly over one shoulder, reached out her spare arm and gathered the miserable mother to her capacious breast.

'I know,' she said sweetly. 'Let the tears come, my darling. Cry it out.'

'He wakes at two in the morning – on the dot!' the woman shrieked into Alice's shoulder. 'And all Stephen does is kick me awake and say "Baby's crying"!'

Alice nodded and swayed on her feet, rocking mother and child at once.

'He hates my milk!' she sobbed. 'I know he does! He makes miserable faces when I try to feed him, and his nappies are filled with brown Camembert! And when I take him down to the clinic all the babies there are on the dreadful artificial milk which stresses their kidneys and makes them sugar addicts. But *they* are all cooing and getting fat, and their mothers stick a bottle in their mouths and go off and have coffee together. And when he's weighed the health visitor just looks at me and says –' she gasped. 'She says . . . s-s-supplementary bottle! It makes me feel so inferior!' She gulped herself to a standstill.

Alice murmured understandingly.

'I know they think I'm not feeding him enough!' she wailed. 'But he looks at me as if he thinks the whole idea is disgusting. And *I* think it's disgusting. I have to mess about with these ghastly bras and these little bits of tissue! And Stephen keeps going on and on about how I should be loving the experience of getting up every half hour! And Stephen's read *all* the books and they all go on and on about African babies being carried all the time, and being breast-fed until they are four, and never getting depressed when they are teenagers because they bonded right. African babies don't get separation anxiety! African babies wean themselves! And when I say I want a drink or a cigarette, or to go out for the evening, he says to me: African babies don't get left with a babysitter!'

'Silver Cross prams!' cried the other mother. 'They sit in their prams, those fat, bottle-fed, happy little things, and smile at me while I lug him about on my back. I was heaving him around like a sack of coal before I even had the stitches out!'

Alice hummed softly and let Mother and baby snivel into each side of her neck.

'Baby-bouncers!' said the first mother, it was like a prayer for release. 'I want a baby-bouncer so I can stick him in it and *leave* him. Just for five minutes!'

'Play-pen!' said the other, like an invocation. 'Just *think* of being allowed a play-pen!'

Alice patted the shorter mother's shoulder with one hand and jiggled the baby on the other arm. She smiled steadily at the other young mother who was nodding wearily and lowering her baby-pack to the ground like Pilgrim getting rid of the fruits of his sins. As soon as the pack touched ground the baby opened his mouth and let out a great bellow of discontent. Both mothers flinched as if they had been struck.

'Now you run along,' Alice said clearly above the noise. The second baby had started up now. The two mothers quivered where they stood like wind-lashed weak-stemmed tulips. 'I'll look after these two. The crèche is ten pounds an hour and we give them massage and flower extracts. You'll see. They'll be new babies when you collect them.'

She took a squalling infant on each hip, and showed the bedraggled mothers out to the orchard. Stephanie watched them approach with huge black eyes in her white face, jogging lightly from one bony foot to another.

Alice waited while they turned up the music and did some warm-up exercises, the usual mimes of stamping down a new-laid lawn, hoeing a flower-bed, and pushing a lawn-mower; and then Stephanie directed them to the garden tools and they put their energy into the real thing.

Alice swayed inside, each baby clinging like a small greedy parasite on a new host.

'Now,' she said, looking from one to another. 'What do you two need?'

She laid them gently on their backs on the kitchen table. At the unknown sensation of being left in a bit of peace both babies contracted their faces and squalled miserably. Alice stepped back a pace and looked at them.

'Floral extracts,' she said to herself, and turned towards the larder.

She came back with a magnum-sized wine bottle stoppered with thick cork. She struggled to open it while the wails from the babies grew louder and more pained. She poured the foaming liquid into a wine glass and took a sip herself. Then carefully, and with patience, she spooned the sparkling clear liquid into each of the hot, wide, noisy mouths.

Both babies were as suddenly silenced as if someone had succumbed to temptation and held a pillow over their heads. The little faces scrunched up while they assessed this new taste which was not dreary old milk nor dull old water, but something dramatically different. Slowly, little toothless beams appeared on their cross faces. Alice spooned in some more, and supported Baby no. 1 as he coughed.

Alice went to the big kitchen cupboard where all sorts of household utensils had been stored, and heaved an old washboard and a wringer out of the way. At the back was a big carriage-built perambulator, massive on bouncy leather straps; more like a landau than a pram. Alice heaved it out, wiped it down, threw in a couple of blankets and sat a baby at each end.

They smiled. They pointed at each other and gurgled. They had seen nothing but their mothers' backs for months, and the change of scenery was welcome. They lay back and watched the sunlight on the kitchen wall. Then they sneezed and giggled at the noise. They had heard nothing but their own mournful bellowing for weeks and their mothers' strained voices. Alice pulled up a chair beside the pram and poured herself another glass from the brown bottle, and gave each baby a sip more.

A party mood was rapidly developing, as the babies goggled around with blue unfocused eyes and Alice joggled the pram with her bare feet. She gave one a tea strainer to look at, and the other a wooden spoon to chew. Both babies accepted these mundane gifts with idiotic enthusiasm. Always before they had been forced to work on brightly coloured educational toys designed to inspire their curiosity, stimulate small-muscle work and develop dexterity. It had really pissed them off. Now they had a chance to get hold of a simple object and hammer the hell out of it on the side of the pram.

It was obviously a big relief. Alice smiled fondly at them both.

Baby no. 2 burped richly and they both creased up as at a dinner-table *bon mot*. Alice giggled too and gave them another spoonful each.

Baby no. 1 started chewing on the handle of the wooden spoon. He drooled blissfully sucking in the impregnated taste of long-ago meals and well-washed wood. Everything at home tasted the same: of sterilizing fluid. This was just great. He cooed.

Outside in the garden the beat of the drum re-minded Alice that the aerobo-work group would shortly be needing tea. She put the kettle on, sway-ing gently and humming to the music.

She had always liked elderflower champagne. You can't beat flower extracts for stress.

The aerobo-work class had a second session after tea, then Alice organized a line of people tossing and catching weights to strengthen the forearms and tighten the chest muscles. The line ran from the wood-shed to the back door of the kitchen. The weights were, of course, logs for the boiler; so that when everyone was hot and sweaty and wanted baths the boiler was stoked and there was plenty of hot water.

Aunty Sarah came downstairs and started a big saucepan of soup for supper, and Alice and the young mothers went into the dining-room for a consultation on getting into harmony with yourself despite distractions.

They left the babies dozing either end of the big perambulator, their cheeks flushed rosy, their little pursed lips puffing out boozy breaths. One of them hiccuped sleepily from time to time like a fat old general dozing after lunch in a London gentleman's club.

Alice started the session with the young mothers with some simple sentence exercises.

'These are called positive affirmations,' she said to them gently. 'You say them every day and very soon they sound right to you – and very soon they become real.'

The two mothers nodded in unison.

'Now, say after me,' Alice commanded sweetly. 'Say "*It's your bloody baby too, you know*".'

'It's your bloody baby too, you know,' the two

women said. Their faces were as blank as if Alice was teaching them Mandarin Chinese.

'*It's your turn to get up and feed him.*'

'It's your turn to get up and feed him,' the women said without expression.

'*I don't care if you* do *have a busy day tomorrow, I have a busy day every day.*'

'I don't care . . .' the women repeated.

'Now louder,' Alice said, 'and with more feeling! "*If you didn't want to look after a baby, you should have told me that a year ago!*"'

'*I don't care if you have got a hangover – it's* still *your turn to get up!*'

'*Just because I'm breast-feeding doesn't mean I'm not sexy!*'

'*I think nappies are disgusting too – you change him!*'

Their voices rose higher, the two young mothers finally twigged that these were sentences which they had wanted to say so badly that they had buried them beyond reach of their voices. Under Alice's smiling permissive coaching they lost their whining tone, they lost their nagging sniping complaints, they stood up straighter . . . and they yelled.

Neither they nor Alice heard the knock at the front door, nor did they hear Michael going to open it. But the man on the doorstep flinched a little as Michael opened the door and three women simultaneously screamed at the tops of their voices:

'GET YOUR ARSE OUT OF BED YOU LAZY SOD!'

'Hello,' Michael said politely.

The vicar shook his head as if he feared that he had hallucinated the Furies shrieking after him. 'Hi!' he said, floundering for his prepared introduction. 'I was just biking past your doorway so I thought I'd call in, see how you're settling in. Don't worry, I'm not checking up on you, or asking you to come to church or anything square or fuddy-duddy like that.'

'Oh,' Michael said. 'Come in.'

Michael led the way into the sitting-room. From the dining-room they could hear an angry monotone: 'Don't you tell me that he has to be carried all the time. If *you* were looking after him you'd bloody well buy a pram – probably a Lamborghini pram! And don't you tell me that you need the car. I need the car. *And* I need a carry-cot, and a carry-cot restraint, *and* I need a high chair, and a play-pen and a baby-bouncer and a buggy. This baby is going to be put down. And don't tell me that African babies are never put down because this,' (with heavy sarcasm) 'this is Sussex where babies are put down, where women need not carry them around all the time. There are no snakes in Sussex. There are no scorpions in Sussex. There are no soldier ants in Sussex. So babies *can* be put down in Sussex. This is Sussex where – I am telling you for the last time – where babies can be put down from time to time and where fathers damn well pull their weight. And I am talking alternate nights here.'

The vicar blinked. 'Have I come at an inconvenient time?' he asked nervously.

Michael waved him to one of Professor Hartley's well-stuffed chesterfield chairs.

'Not at all,' he said pleasantly.

The vicar glanced around nervously. 'I thought I heard someone shouting,' he said tentatively.

'DON'T TALK TO ME ABOUT BONDING!' came an almighty scream from the dining-room.

'Not especially,' Michael said, smiling vaguely.

'Great,' the vicar said. 'Not especial shouting. Great. Great place. Good to see some young people living in the country.'

Michael nodded gently, but said nothing. In the dining-room a long eerie scream collapsed into a howl, and then tears. Michael raised his eyebrows interrogatively at the vicar who blinked rapidly.

'I really worry about second home ownership and young people being driven into the Inner Cities,' he said in a rush. 'That's why I'm so glad to see some young people here. I'm really glad that the Church is at last responding in a positive way to that challenge. I'm just here because I couldn't get an appointment to work in Toxteth, but I keep hoping.'

'WHAT I WANT IS SOME SEX!' came a deep sibilant whisper from the dining-room.

The vicar jumped instinctively and then gave an embarrassed little laugh. 'Nothing special?' he checked with Michael.

Michael smiled gently and shook his head. Michael felt *so cool* he could not speak for his sense of deep hipness.

The vicar ploughed on. 'I mean, I'm not sure if there is a God or not – I don't think anyone can ever be really sure. But if there is a God, and if he has some kind of personal plan for people in general that is, then he must have a personal plan for me.'

He broke off and a worried expression crossed his face. 'I don't know if I'm making sense here,' he said. 'I'm just speculating aloud, you see. I mean, if you were to tell me that you have no sense of a God as an intervening force in human affairs – I can't really argue about that.'

Michael smiled. He did not look likely to raise the issue of an interventionist deity at any time in the next four years.

'I WANT TO BE CRUSHED IN A PAS-SIONATE EMBRACE!' the voice from the dining-room said.

This time, the vicar totally ignored the interruption. 'Now, I can't go all the way there,' he confessed. 'I can't see God really worrying personally about every single one of us. I just can't visualize it. But if there *was* a personal God like that, then I suppose he wants me to work here for a while – and not go to Toxteth. If he's aware of me as an individual with a career plan, that is,' he said thoughtfully. 'He could, of course, be aware of me as an individual unit without being aware of my small petty life plans. Or she, of course. I said "he" for God but I really should have said he-she; or she-he.'

He caught himself up. 'Hey! I'm sorry! I never

usually talk to people about God. I reckon no one wants to hear a clergyman going on and on about God all the time.'

Michael gazed at him, utterly blank.

'I never wear the clerical collar,' the vicar offered. 'Today I had to wear it – because I was doing a funeral for one of the older residents of the village, and they like the old bell, book and candle stuff, you know. But most of the time I just go round in jeans and a sweatshirt. Just like any ordinary person really, because that's what I am. Just an ordinary sinner, like any ordinary sinner.' He spread his hands wide in a deprecating gesture and nodded urgently at Michael.

'I WISH HE WOULD TAKE ME TO BED AND DO IT LIKE HE MEANS IT!' came a penetrating hiss from the dining-room. The vicar was deaf to all interruptions.

'Oh! There I go again!' he said playfully. He put out one hand and jovially slapped himself. 'Talking about sin! I didn't *really* mean sin, I meant failing to treat others and yourself in a caring sort of way.'

He paused and smiled at Michael with gap-toothed sincerity. 'I think that's what we mean when we say sin. These days we have this humanist approach – no one wants to hear about sin any more. Stupid old-fashioned word, really. I never use it. You know, I just don't have a concept of commandments and breaking them. In the modern-day Church we are much more interested in the notion of psychology and motive, you know. Not so much what one does, but what one meant to do, or what one would do if one could.' He paused for a moment. 'And of course why one stops. What is stopping one, or if one is stopping oneself. If you see what I mean.'

Michael nodded. His mother was Roman Catholic, attending mass only when she felt especially vindictive towards his father and wanted to go to confession and moan about him. His father meanwhile played golf on Sunday mornings with an evangelical enthusiasm, and so Michael's previous acquaintance with the Anglican clergy was slight.

He knew of course that the Anglican Church is dedicated to exploring such deep and important theological questions as whether it is worse to have a fairy for a vicar than to have a woman. Overall, as far as Michael knew, the Church has ruled that a fairy is the lesser of the two evils. It's all right to have a fairy for a vicar as long as he doesn't sleep with anybody. He can be a fairy but not a *practising* fairy. A sort of theoretical fairy, a fairy-in-permanent-waiting. A fairy in limbo. A laid-up fairy.

But nothing can redeem a woman from being a woman. Either you are a woman or you are not. You can't really *be* a woman without being a practising woman. Michael was ignorant of the numbers of deaconesses in the Anglican Church who are giving it a good try . . .

These complex theological points were of little interest to Michael, and this vicar was of little interest too. But he was a polite boy and did his mother credit by sitting nicely in the chair and waiting for the vicar to leave.

'Now, I know that you are living here with a woman,' the vicar said. His smile was intended to convey a broadminded acceptance of changing styles.

'WHY DOESN'T HE RIP MY CLOTHES OFF?' came from the dining-room in a Lorelei-howl.

Michael looked at the vicar and wondered why this stranger should be so familiar with Michael's domestic arrangements and why he was smiling as he described them. Michael's hackles rose slightly. Did this strange man find Michael living with Alice somehow funny?

'So I just wanted you to know that though there are some real old-fashioned people here who are stuck on all the discarded morality – you know – marriage and chastity and sin and redemption – well, I'm not like that, and you won't meet anyone like that at our church. You're welcome at any time to come and take part in our services.'

Michael blinked. 'I don't think we believe really . . .' he said vaguely, thinking of Alice and the Great Earth Mother and what the two of Them would say about going to church.

The vicar spread his hands. 'Oh no!' he said. 'Nobody believes these days, we all doubt. It's healthy! And no one reads the Bible or the old prayers, of course. We just have a coming together with a few songs with guitars from the youth group, of course, and then we all shake each other's hands and then we go up to the end of the church and have a bit of bread and wine – we don't call it communion or anything – don't think you're getting into any out-of-date mumbo-jumbo here! And then the real part begins when we have coffee at the back of the church and we get together as a group of people with shared doubts and uncertainties. I see it as more a community than a church. It's really great!'

'I'll ask,' Michael said feebly, going to the door. He hadn't been to church for some time, but the memory he had of it was not that of a coffee morning made especially hideous by amateur young guitar players. 'I'll get her.'

'You need not get her! She is Here!' Alice said, throwing open the door and sweeping into the room.

She had changed her dress since the babies had been sick on her shoulder and now she was wearing a long flowing purple sari. The brilliant gold hem swept the floor, the loose end, woven with gold thread, was flung carelessly over her shoulder. Her long black hair was combed free over her shoulders, a gold band tied across her forehead. Her breath, panting with passion, smelled sweetly of the elder-flower champagne which had worked such wonders with the babies.

Even Michael, who was accustomed to her dress-style, gaped. The vicar, who was not, goggled, stepped sharply backwards, stumbled on a footstool and saved himself with a wild grab for the mantelpiece.

'I know your sort!' Alice said to him with unconcealed loathing. 'I've met your sort before. You're cocktail vicars, you are. A little bit of this and a little bit of that. A little bit of reincarnation and a little bit of Buddhism. A little bit of meditation and a little bit of psychiatry. A little bit of counselling training, enough to muddle people up, and a bit of humanism and liberalism. A lot of tolerance towards other religions because we're all worshipping the same God, aren't we? And a lot of sneering and unkindness to the old ladies on the flower rota who want to decorate the church and have a crib at Christmas. Sliced loaf for communion bread, and water instead of wine. Sweaters in the pulpit and the office hours in the vicarage.'

The vicar gaped and clung to the mantelpiece as if it were a spar in a stormy sea.

'No wonder people want magic!' Alice thundered. 'No wonder people want revivals! No wonder people want fundamentalism! They ask you for bread and you don't even have the conviction to give them a stone. You give them Play-Doh!'

Michael gasped. She was magnificent.

The vicar gave up clinging to the mantelpiece and sank to the floor at her feet. Alice spurned him with her sandalled foot. At least, she stuck out her toe and gave him a prod, if that is what 'spurning' means.

'I have more spirituality in my morning cup of tea than you have in the whole of a Sunday!' she said disdainfully. 'And you come around here pretending you are just biking past, to try and sell us this mish-mash of watered down half-heartedness! Good God! I should be ashamed of you if I was Jesus!'

The vicar gave a pitiful little wail and buried his face in his hands. Alice looked down at him, unrelenting.

'Yes, I would weep if I were you,' she said fiercely. 'No one has a clue what you think or what you mean. You don't even have the guts to stick to a faith which has lasted two thousand years. You have to muck it about and dress it up and pretend that it's trendy.'

Despite her anger, her voice softened at that. Two thousand years, to a priestess of the Old Faith of the Great Mother, is chicken-feed – but Alice was too generous to taunt him with it. Between Alice and the Great Mother the vicar represented a passing phase, pathetic in its temporary nature – a kind of Jesus-come-lately.

'You have to mash up your faith, and mix it up so that it blends with silly little fads which won't last two seconds,' she said. 'No wonder people don't go to church. They can get that sort of stuff at evening classes!'

The vicar broke into a deep bellow of grief and sobbed into the hessian weave of Professor Hartley's sofa. Alice tossed the end of her sari over her shoulder and stepped back a little.

They waited. Michael looked at Alice for prompting. When Mrs Wheatley had cried like this they had charged her thirty pounds to do 'YOU KNOW WHAT'. But he was not sure how to do that with a clergyman. He would not know quite where to start.

Alice did not look at him, her eyes rested on the vicar and she stood with her head on one side, listening. His sobs showed no signs of abating, indeed they steadied into a rolling bawl. He sounded as if he were settling in for a good weep.

Michael cleared his throat nervously. 'What shall we do with him?' he asked in an undertone.

'Leave him to cry and charge him twenty-five pounds as he leaves,' Alice said softly. 'He's a vicar, he understands about tithing. And set an extra place for supper. They always stay for tea, you'd think vicarages came without a kettle.'

'Oh,' Michael said. It wasn't like this for Catholics.

The vicar's name was Maurice and he had second and third helpings of soup.

That was a mistake, for Stephanie, who was learning to cook under Alice's negligent tuition, had sliced some of the red mushrooms into it and it was spicey and slightly hallucinogenic. Everyone got very relaxed and friendly sitting around the kitchen table, and the vicar did balancing tricks with the glasses.

Aunty Sarah watched him with her bright dark eyes. 'Never visited me before then,' she said sharply.

Maurice looked at her, without recognition. 'Are you one of my parishioners?' he asked. He giggled delightedly. 'One of my little flock?' he asked. 'One of my little flockers?'

Stephanie stared at him with her huge black eyes.

Alice cocked her head. 'There's a car coming up the drive,' she said. 'Anyone expecting someone?'

They all shook their heads. The young mothers were struggling home on the bus together, Stephanie was staying the night. Gary, Timofy and Jonafon would drive home in Gary's Mini.

'Yes, I am one of your parishioners all right!' Aunty Sarah said with some of her old malice. 'But I never saw hide nor hair of you before!'

There was a sharp knock on the back door, Alice got up from the table and flung it open. The sweet smell of the dark spring night wafted into the kitchen, the onion and garlic and magic mushroom smell wafted out.

Two pale faces stared in at them.

'Excuse us intruding,' the woman said in a sharp unapologetic voice. 'We've not been introduced . . . but my husband's bike has been leaning against your gate since two forty-three this afternoon. Is Maurice still here?'

She was a pale-haired, pale-faced woman, about Alice's age, with a mouth set in a narrow weary line. She wore her hair scraped back in a half ponytail on the back of her head. Her companion was an older woman with blue-rinsed hair and sharp grey eyes. She took a little step forwards so that she could see the kitchen more clearly.

Maurice giggled. 'My wife!' he said. 'Ssshh! My wife! Ooops! My wife! I forgot I was due home for tea!'

He stood up, but the bench caught him at the back of the knees and felled him instantly.

'I'm Anne Mayberry,' the vicar's wife said to Alice, taking in every detail of the purple sari, the long dark flowing hair, and the inane beaming face of Maurice over his empty soup plate. 'And this is Patricia Simmonds. You met her husband the day you moved in, Doctor Simmonds.'

'Oh yes,' Alice said. 'Hello.'

Both women were scenting the air like well-trained bloodhounds. They could smell the tang of Stephanie's soup, they could scent gossip and scandal and untoward doings.

Maurice disentangled himself from the bench and started saying his farewells. The two women hovered in the doorway, longing to cross the threshold but not daring to step over without invitation. Alice's welcoming smile had died on her lips. She was watching them, her face guarded.

'Goodnight everybody,' Maurice said. 'I've had a love, I've had a love, I've had a love-love-lovely time. Goodbye Michael, goodbye Stephanie, goodbye Janet, goodbye Gary and Timofy, goodbye Maureen, goodbye Jonafon.' He came to Aunty Sarah and paused. 'I am sorry, I don't remember your name,' he said.

Aunty Sarah gleamed wickedly at him. 'Sarah,' she said. 'Miss Coulter to you.'

'Goodbye Sarah, Miss Coulter-Tooyew,' Maurice continued impenetrably high. He floated towards the back door and, ignoring the icy glare of his wife, clasped Alice's broad white hand in his own. 'I can't tell you what a meaningful exchange we have just had,' he said. 'This really has been a challenge and an exploration for me. I feel reborn. I feel deeply satisfied by my experience with you. I've had a love, I've had a love, I've had a love-love-lovely evening.'

Alice disengaged herself with rare tact, glancing towards Anne Mayberry who was taking in every detail of her husband's appearance from the undone clerical collar to the eyes still red from weeping, and his born-again beaming face.

'It was nice to meet you,' Alice said formally. She nodded at the pair of sphinxes on the doorstep. 'How kind of you to call. Please come again,' she said.

'Running some kind of club here, are you?' Patricia Simmonds asked sharply. 'I see people coming and going at all hours. I live opposite, you see. I never pry, I'm not that sort of person. But my kitchen faces out this way and there's such a lot of traffic in and out of your drive the past two days. Not like it used to be when the old lady was alive. I can't help noticing.'

'We are running a growth centre for people who need spiritual or physical help,' Alice said smoothly.

Patricia's eyes were bright with curiosity. 'Perhaps you'd better have a talk with my husband,' she said. 'He's very down on all that amateur medicine stuff,' she laughed, a thin insincere cackle. 'Witchcraft he calls it!'

Alice did not laugh with her. 'So do I,' she said.

'Goodbye again,' Maurice said. Alice smiled her farewell to him and to the sharp faces of the two women. They all three walked across the courtyard to the Mayberrys' old Volvo car when Maurice suddenly stopped.

'Did she say Miss Coulter?' he demanded. His feet wove quickly in and out of each other's path and his wife slipped an arm around his waist.

'She said Miss Coulter!' he exclaimed. 'The old lady! But she's dead. I have her funeral booked for next week! Yet I saw her having her tea!'

Both women stopped abruptly.

'Did you say Miss Coulter was there?' Patricia Simmonds demanded.

'I saw. I saw. I saw. I sought I saw her,' Maurice said.

'You're drunk,' Anne Mayberry said between clenched teeth. 'Get in the car, I'm driving.'

'No, wait!' Patricia said. 'There's something funny going on!'

She turned back towards the house and took two steps towards the open kitchen door. Alice, standing in the doorway, straining her ears to hear the slurred tones of Maurice, saw the brightness of

Patricia's made-up face and the sudden delight in her eyes.

'I say . . .' Patricia cried.

Alice quickly shut the back door.

SUNDAY

Alice passed a restless night. There was something in the bright hard eyes of Mrs Simmonds which gave her an uneasy feeling. Even a handful of fresh Michael's essences could not smooth away the worry lines on her forehead that were so irritatingly clear in the mirror that morning. Alice confronted herself in the dressing-table mirror while Michael slumbered in bed behind her. Rumpled in sleep he looked like a boy of sixteen. Alice repressed a flicker of irritation at all that taut epidermis and rapid metabolic rate being wasted on young people who do nothing with their skin except squeeze spots out of it.

Aunty Sarah was downstairs brewing tea. 'Someone phoned for you from the university,' she said. 'Some writers' circle, coming here.'

'Oh God!' said Alice. 'I had forgotten!'

The Suffix University writers' circle met monthly in members' houses. Alice had joined on the advice of Mrs Bland during the heyday of marital counselling when Mrs Bland, prompted by Charles, thought that Alice should take her energies and her powers of analysis elsewhere. She told Alice that she had talent. She encouraged her to join the writers' circle in search of an audience who would (unlike her husband) occasionally listen to her. Alice was attracted by the idea of describing, barely veiled with fictional names and in intimate detail, Charles's many failures as a husband. She wrote, with little skill but much suppressed venom, some dramatic Plath-like poetry about entrapment, enslavement, and being married to Hitler, A. or Napoleon, B.

Within months this had palled; but Alice, suffering from loyalty and inertia, never shed the habit of wasting a Sunday morning once a month. It was Alice's turn to play host and she had barely time to defrost another carrot cake before they arrived. It was a large turn-out, inspired by literature and driven by the quite astounding rumours which were murmuring their way around the university about Alice Hartley's new address.

'Alice, darling!' said the first one through the door, her horn-rimmed spectacles sweeping the hall. She was Mary Hutchinson, the natural leader of the group, who had published a romantic war novel in 1942 when patriotism had obscured the lack of literary merit. With her came George Groves (*The Life and Works of George Finnegan Blakemore Groves* in three volumes, 1972, as yet unpublished), Sarah Finlay (*Cry the Bright Star Downhill – and Uphill Again*, unpublished collection of prose-poems), and Barbara Wray (*Nurse Babs and Heartbreak Hospital*,

Nurse Babs on Holiday, Nurse Babs and the Hi-jack, Nurse Babs and the Plane Crash, Nurse Babs Alone in the Jungle, Nurse Babs and the Cannibal Islanders, Nurse Babs in Big Trouble, published by True Life Love Stories 1975, 1980, 1981, 1982, 1983, 1984, 1985).

Alice was pouring the herbal tea and slicing carrot cake when the others arrived: Piers Winterman (*Little Men with Big Tools: Ten Years with the Gurkhas, Mutiny in the Ranks: Five Extra Years with the Gurkhas, The End of Glory: A Commander's Thoughts on Being Ordered to Leave his Gurkhas, The Gurkha's Great Mistake: A Transcript of the Court Martial of a Gurkha Officer who Rightly Refused to Abandon his Command*); Piers had brought Letty Finch (*Dithering Heights: A Novel of Uncertainty Set in Yorkshire, Far from the Irritating Crowd* and *June the Obscure*); two new members of the group came together, Sylvia Hayward ('Writer's Block', an unfinished poem), and Claud Church (*Blood!, Rage!, Sweat!, Bother!* published by Macho Books 1965, 1966, 1967, 1968).

'Come in! Come in!' said Alice gaily, showing them into the sitting-room. Mary Hutchinson and Barbara Wray noted with one eager glance the familiar sight of Professor Hartley's hessian-covered suite and Professor Hartley's recliner-rocker chair in the unfamiliar surroundings.

Alice passed plates heavy with leaden lumps of carrot cake. Piers Winterman, who had once soldered his dentures to his gums for forty-eight hours with Alice Hartley's carrot cake, repressed a grunt of disappointment.

Alice poured caffeine-free coffee while Mary called the meeting to order.

'At our last meeting we all agreed to write a little piece – I call them fugitive pieces – about our earliest memory,' she said.

Piers Winterman came out of a reverie of thick gateaux fearlessly bitten in early years, with a start. 'Eh? I don't remember,' he said.

Barbara Wray looked earnest. 'That's very significant,' she said. 'Not remembering your earliest memory. Very significant! What they call a Freudian slip.'

'I suggest we all read ours, and share some positive and helpful criticism,' Mary said. 'Shall I start?'

Since no one had the courage to shout 'no' and flee from the room, Mary pulled a loose-leaf folder from her shoulder bag and turned the coloured pages. Mary, as a professional author, colour-coded her work to match what she called her 'market' by which she meant magazine editors too tired, too drunk, or too lacking in taste to tell her to take her outdated and ungrammatical drivel elsewhere.

'Fugitive piece,' she announced relentlessly.

> '*My earliest memory.*
>
> *It is not how it used to be,*
> *The swing which swung from the apple tree,*
> *The clock which stood at ten to three*
> *On Linden Lea.*

If I could go back there I would–
Where Nanny smiled when I was good,
And life held promises, just as it should–
Be, Linden Lea.'

Mary stopped with a deep sigh, as if the emotions aroused by her poem were too deep to bear. Then she raised her eyes and looked around the silent circle with a smile of quiet complacency.

'Now tell me!' she said confidently. 'You know I always say that the way to learn is to listen to criticism!' She opened her hands. 'Tear me to shreds!' she invited.

'I think it's very significant – very Freudian!' Barbara Wray said breathlessly. 'Really good. I so wish I could write like you do, Mary.'

'Excellent!' said Piers Winterman. 'Reminds me of something. I don't quite remember what.'

Mary nodded. 'Who was it said: we love great art because it reminds us of other great art?' she asked rhetorically.

No one answered.

'It's a b-b-bit s-soft for my taste,' Claud offered. Mary turned on him a look which was as soft as an ice-pick. He choked on a non-existent crumb of carrot cake and hid his face in a teacup.

'Soft?' Mary enquired glacially. 'Tell me more!'

'It's a w-w-w-woman's poem,' he said, grasping at biological determinism and inarguable truth. 'It's a woman's p-p-p-poem.'

Mary glowed. 'Yes, indeed,' she said. 'It is. Alice?'

Alice had been thinking about Patricia Simmonds and the flint-faced vicar's wife. It was coffee time in every kitchen in England – dissection time for the reputation of all village dwellers. Alice knew that either in the house opposite – where Patricia Simmonds barely glanced out of her kitchen window, never pried, and yet acted as census gatherer for the whole lane – or in the vicarage kitchen, her name would be mentioned, her relationship with Michael discussed, and the vicar's hallucination of dead Aunty Sarah at the supper table would be thoroughly explored.

'I'm sorry, she said with a start. 'I was miles away!'

'Shall I read it again?' Mary asked eagerly.

'No! No!' Alice said hastily. 'I heard the poem. Tell me, Mary, what is Linden Lea?'

It was questions like that which had Alice's welcome in the writers' circle balanced on a knife edge.

'What is Linden Lea?' Mary cried incredulously. 'What is Linden Lea?'

Alice nodded.

'Why!' Mary tinkled. 'Everyone knows that, Alice. You *really* must make an effort to read a little more poetry. But come now! We can't waste the whole meeting on my little effort. What have *you* written, Alice?'

Alice shook her head. 'I have been so busy moving

I have had no time to write at all,' she said. She looked apologetic but her heart was singing. 'The days when I needed you dreary lot to fill in my Sunday mornings are long gone,' she said to herself. 'In fact,' she said out loud, 'I really fear I shall have to resign as an active member of the writers' circle. I am *so* busy these days.'

There were a few murmurs of regret at the prospect of losing an audience for their writings, but a general sense of relief at having lost a rival. The Suffix University writers' circle – like many others – hovered on a knife edge of competitive hatred of each other, and solidarity and support against an unreceptive world.

'Shall I read?' Barbara Wray asked. The others nodded and she fluttered the pages of her pink notepaper pad.

'*Little Babs Wray had a golden-furred teddy to match the counterpane of yellow,*' she said. '*Even when she was a woman, Babs would always remember the girlish prettiness of her childhood home. She could not explain that feeling to Doctor Hinchley. He would have laughed her to scorn! Doctor Hinchley had no time for sentiment, for memories. Doctor Hinchley was a surgical instrument.*

'"*He feels nothing," Staff Nurse Smith told Babs. "Every nurse in this hospital would lay down her life for him! But he has eyes for no one. All he ever thinks about is his work!*"

'*Babs smiled. One day perhaps, he would see her for the girl she was . . .*'

Barbara Wray broke off. 'There's quite a lot more,' she said. 'But perhaps that gives you the idea of the way I am working. It's a whole new departure for me, a much more Freudian approach. You see, I am looking at the childhood of Nurse Babs this time. That's a much more psychological approach than I have ever taken before.'

Alice nodded, smiling. She was far away. Last night Michael had shown her what Mrs Wheatley meant by 'YOU KNOW WHAT'. Alice had been surprised at the extent of Mrs Wheatley's girlhood reading, even if the book had been upside down.

There was a murmur of appreciation for Barbara Wray's earliest memory. No one could criticize Barbara who had published, repeatedly, and they had not. Only Mary raised the question of whether this was a fugitive piece entitled 'My earliest memory' or, in fact, the start of a new Nurse Babs novel – and thus outside the remit of today's session.

Barbara opened her blue eyes very wide and shrugged her shoulders. 'Who knows?' she said sweetly. 'When the Muse is upon me – I follow where she leads.'

'I s-s-suppose I'm outside the r-r-remit too,' Claud volunteered. He flipped open his notepad and started to read in a staccato shout with no trace of his stammer:

'Brett jammed the machine-gun trigger down as far as it would go and watched the targets jump and

*splinter through the cross of the night-sight. It re-
minded him of his earliest memory when he had been a
little boy walking beside the pond in the park and
watching the ducks. Then, too, he had been mad with
anger towards the ducks. Every crust he had thrown
them had been a bull's eye on a duckling's head. His
score never fell below 100 per cent. They had said of
him then, as they said of him now . . . He never
misses . . .'*

Claud broke off. 'I th-th-thought it might turn
into a new n-n-n-novel,' he said. 'I th-th-thought I
might call it . . . *Duck!*'

'Duck?' asked Alice, momentarily coming out of
her reverie.

'A sort of p- a sort of p- a sort of pun,' he explained.

'Oh,' Alice said, losing interest again.

'And my p-p-publishers like short titles,' he
said. Everyone who had large, unbound manuscripts hidden in cardboard boxes in the broom
cupboard flinched at the casual ownership of 'my
publishers'.

'They like titles like *Rage!* and *Blood!* and *Sweat!*'
Claud said. 'I thought *Duck!* would be another good
one.'

'But right outside the remit of today's meeting,'
Mary said swiftly. 'If no one has anything which
addresses the topic, I actually wrote another poem I
can offer you.'

'I wrote something,' Letty Finch said quickly.
She cleared her throat and began.

'By the side of Worthing Pier
By the shining big-sea water,
Played all day beside the shallows,
All day long beside the shallows,
Little Letty in her bathers.

Watched the seagulls eating crisp-packs
Learned their names, and all their secrets,
Paddled in the outfall water,
Letty in the outfall water!
Catching typhus and e. coli.'

Lettice broke off – 'I stopped there,' she said. 'But I think it has a certain rhythm, don't you?'

'Typhus?' Barbara asked incredulously. 'E. coli?' She smiled and leaned forward and tapped Letty on the knee. 'When you've been writing doctor–nurse novels as long as I have you will know that the one thing you *never* mention is disease or medicine. The readers just *won't* take it.'

'Hardly poetic topics!' Mary tinkled. Mary knew that poetic topics were about Linden Lea, and the village swains, and children like little angels with eyes as blue as the sky praying, like as not, at the foot of their tiny truckle beds.

'It's Green,' Letty Finch said defiantly. 'People ought to know! There is an epidemic just waiting in the outfall of sewers, I was going to go on and take it all in – dolphins, whales, oil spills, the greenhouse effect. I think poetry should campaign!'

Alice nodded, smiling. There had been a time

when she too had thought poetry should campaign. There had been a time when she too had tried to make 'ozone layer' rhyme or scan – either, she had been past caring. But now she stretched with the sensuality of an overfed cat, now Alice had finished with words. She believed in primordial rhythms and non-verbal, but hyperactive, body language.

Piers grunted. 'Reminds me of something I used to know at school,' he volunteered. 'Here, I'll read you mine.

'*First thing I remember is Pa lashing into me with six of the best. Good thing too. He must have caught me doing something that was out of line. And that's how you treat children, catch them young, train them up, and don't spare the rod. Very like dealing with natives too. When I was in the Gurkhas we used to say "catch them young, train them up, and don't spare the rod." Why, I remember . . .*'

'Gracious, is that the time?' Mary interrupted. 'Piers, we have to break into your reading here, I have to go and I am sure Alice has a thousand and one things to do.'

Alice nodded and smiled. Everyone got to their feet and packed their manuscripts away in their bags with scrupulous care. There was a sense of euphoria which came from relief of the ever-present fear that someone would criticize – or worse still, praise and then pinch your writing.

'Theme for next month!' Mary cried above the noise. 'My happiest moment!'

Piers nodded. 'That's easy!' he said. 'When I was

commissioned. You'll be sorry to miss that,' he said to Alice.

Alice nodded. 'I will,' she lied convincingly. 'My happiest moment!' she said thoughtfully. She looked at the group of talentless, joyless plagiarists with an indulgent eye. The merest glimpse of Alice's recent happy moments would have shocked them senseless. 'I will join you again as soon as I get settled here and then I shall have all these treats to look forward to!' Alice said kindly.

She shepherded them out into the hall but Babs Wray lingered behind the rest. The others straggled out into their cars, and Babs hovered on the doorstep.

'I hear you've left the Professor?' she asked, her gerbil face screwed up in pretended sympathy, her voice an avid whisper. 'Don't keep it all to yourself, Alice, you must talk it out. Otherwise it's just all too Freudian.'

'I've left him,' Alice confirmed coolly. The billowing sleeves of her blue gown were like huge rolling waves threatening to sweep Babs out of the house and away; but she clung to the doorpost like a determined barnacle facing the spring tides.

'You *must* talk it through!' she declared. Babs was starving for gossip. Her eyes were bright with insincere sympathy. 'I *know* how badly he treated you, Alice, all these years I have seen it! I have longed to speak before but now you can confide in me without reserve!' She slid an arm around Alice's soft waist and hugged her, as if she would squeeze words out.

'Tell me, dear!' she said. 'You can tell me everything!'

'Not much to tell really,' Alice said cheerily, unwrapping the arm as if it were an apron string.

'I hear he left you,' Babs said. 'You know me, I never gossip – but everyone is saying that he has run off with Miranda Bloomfeather – one of his students!'

'No,' Alice said, her smile hardening.

'*Don't* cut yourself off like this!' Babs pleaded. 'Tell me what is happening, Alice! Share your troubles with me!'

Alice detached Babs's hand, which was clinging to the doorknob, and with infinite gentleness shoved her off the doorstep.

'I left him,' she said. Babs was thrust towards the car by the mere force of Alice's unstoppable will and a hand in the small of her back. Babs's feet moved away while her eyes boggled backwards.

'*I* left *him*,' Alice repeated with emphasis.

Babs goggled over her shoulder as Alice propelled her towards the car.

'But why?' she asked. 'He's a Professor, and head of department, Alice! Why leave? He has tenure!'

Alice opened the car door. Babs's little hands fastened on the blue billowing sleeve.

'I thought you were so happy, Alice,' she said. 'I thought you had everything a woman could want! Why leave?'

Alice pressed Babs in her pudgy stomach at the same time as leaning on her shoulder. Babs folded abruptly in the middle and Alice thrust her backwards into the passenger seat of the car.

'Because he was a rotten lay,' Alice said in her clear ringing voice. 'Tell everyone, Babs. He was a rotten lay and always had been.'

Babs emitted a short scream of shock.

Alice smiled benignly and slammed the car door. Mary Hutchinson, whose ears had been waggling like a satellite tracking aerial, was white with shock. George Groves, in the back seat with Sarah Finlay, looked blankly at Alice.

'Goodbye,' Alice called, waving her broad white hand. 'Goodbye.'

Michael was waiting for her in the kitchen, wearing only his blue jeans, blinking owlishly into the steam of a cup of decaffeinated coffee. Alice looked at his skinny naked chest and felt her desires smouldering.

'I'd have thought you might have encouraged them to join a class and grow?' he remarked.

'No,' Alice said. 'They don't need therapy, they have their writing. If their life is unfulfilling they just write about a better one.'

Michael looked surprised. He had been studying English Literature for some time now but the idea of authorship as a prolonged fantasy, without emission other than words, was a new one to him.

'Do *all* authors do that?' he asked.

'Oh yes,' Alice said. 'They just pretend that things are how they want them to be.'

'And readers like this?' Michael asked, surprised.

'No one ever asks them,' Alice said wisely. 'I

should think they hate it, but if they want something better then they have to write it themselves, and then they're not readers any more but writers. Then they *have* to say they like each other's books. That's what is meant by the literary élite.'

Michael looked at her with profound admiration. 'Alice,' he said, 'I never really understood English Literature before. Thank you.'

Alice looked at his concave chest and his thin arms, his warm brown puppyish eyes and the interesting convex curve in his jeans.

'Come upstairs and thank me,' she said temptingly. 'I'll tell you all about Beowulf.'

Alice and Michael rolled around on Professor Hartley's posture-sprung bed with the relaxed sensuality of established lovers. The sunlight streamed through the windows, outside the birds cheeped encouragement to their nestlings and, perhaps, even to Michael and Alice, whose naked coupling bodies may have appeared like remarkably large and wriggley worms. Sometimes Michael was on top, pitching and rolling on Alice's energetic heaves – a sensation very like masturbating on a lilo in stormy seas. Sometimes Michael was beneath her, struggling with a sensation near terror when she sat up and then bounced enthusiastically up and down like a new plump recruit to the Pony Club, hell-bent on mastering the rhythm of the rising trot on a skinny Shetland. Sometimes Michael lay absolutely still as Alice swarmed over him, his slight body engulfed by her ample curves and folds, sometimes he whimpered as she ground the bony cusp of her pelvis on his. Alice paid no attention – neither to his seasickness, nor to his brief cries of pain. She hummed – a deep burbling sound which came from low in the smooth white column of her throat, and rolled easily and triumphantly from one obscure sexual position to another. Her black almond-shaped eyes were closed, her dark hair tumbled about her serene face as she bobbed and rocked with Michael gibbering between pleasure and pain underneath her. She threw her arms around Michael and flung herself sideways towards the mattress, rolling as she went, so that Michael would bob up on top. However, Michael's slight weight was insufficient counterbalance to Alice's heavier momentum – she misjudged the distance and they crashed off the bed to the floor, Alice landing hard on her back with Michael, gripping like a baby koala to its Mum, on top of her.

Alice let out a delighted giggle. 'Michael, you beast!' she said breathlessly. 'Oh God, I love it when you treat me rough! Take me!'

Michael nearly asked 'where?' but caught the question back in the nick of time. Inexperienced he may have been just a few short days ago – but he had enjoyed an intensive course in Alice's sexual appetites and he recognized certain keywords. For instance, when Mrs Hartley begged him 'don't hurt me!' that was his cue to slap her very gently on her firm, rounded flanks. This was a process which had to be undertaken with a certain amount of caution. On one occasion Michael's enthusiasm had overtaken his innate gentleness and he had slapped too hard whereupon Alice had dealt him a blow which made his head ring. Thereafter Michael understood that his image as a brutal male was largely symbolic.

But when Alice said 'take me!' there could be no confusion. It was an invitation for rapid thrusting movements in whichever direction seemed appropriate. And when she said, screamed, or whispered 'oh yes, yes, yes', Michael could relax with the satisfaction of a job well done and reward himself with the rapid gallop into his own release.

Michael, clinging to Mrs Hartley's bucking body as she breathed 'take me', cast his mind back to his glossary of sexual terms and obediently bounced up and down very quick. He found this process so exquisitely enjoyable that it was difficult, indeed nigh impossible, to bear in mind that he *must* continue doing this until Mrs Hartley screamed 'OH! YES! YES! YES!' Michael only knew one way to achieve this. While Mrs Hartley throatily groaned, 'Oh, take me, take me!' Michael tunefully started the refrain: 'Ten green bottles . . .'

By never wavering in his concentration on the tune *and* the necessary arithmetic, working from ten green bottles hanging on the wall, down to nine, eight, seven, six, and so on, and by bumping and thrusting in remorseless time (bear in mind that Michael started the song adagio, built up through allegro, and then concluded allegretto spirito! and falsetto too, actually), Mrs Hartley reached total satisfaction with a scream of 'OH! YES! YES! YES!' just as Michael trilled, 'And there'll be *four* green bottles hanging on the wall! . . . Oh God!'

Aunty Sarah, who was pretending to dust the banister for all of this performance with a reminiscent smile on her face, nodded her old head wisely.

Michael and Alice lay still for a while enjoying the dreamy peace of post-coital content. It says much for their sexual compatibility that they had never got further than four green bottles. And it says much for Michael's concern for Alice's sexual happiness that he had chosen 'Ten green bottles' in the first place. The consequences of, say, 'Three blind mice' would not have been nearly so happy.

'Oh!' Alice sighed at last. She sat up and threw the heavy waves of her black hair away from her face and over her shoulders. 'I must get up,' she said. 'There's a few people coming today and I have to prepare.'

Michael felt for the bed behind him and crawled up to it like Sherpa Tenzing making the peak of Everest without oxygen.

'Phew!' he said. He rested, panting for a few moments until he had caught his breath. 'Who's coming?' he asked.

'Aerobo-garden Workshop at midday, Mothers and Babies at two, Women's Rights at four, and in the evening I thought we might have a collective meeting to get in tune with ourselves and each other again,' Alice said.

'Again?' Michael asked. He could not remember a collective meeting on attunement.

Alice smiled. 'Like last time,' she said. 'Herbal tobacco and lots of sex.'

'Oh, *that* attunement meeting!' Michael said. 'Do you need me here during the day? I should really go in to the university to meet my Sunday reading group at midday.'

'You run along,' Alice said kindly. 'Take the car if you want.'

Michael, who had just been getting up, collapsed back on the pillows, quite pale. 'Your husband would be bound to see it,' he said. 'I wouldn't want to upset him unnecessarily . . . I wouldn't really . . . He might . . .'

'Yes,' Alice said. 'OK. I'll run you in now, if you like.'

'I'll get a lift back with the Mothers and Babies,' Michael said.

Alice nodded and pulled on a dress over her rumpled head. It was deep royal blue, with a hem trimmed with gold sequins and embroidered with golden stars and silver moons. It was one of her favourite dresses, as yet almost unworn. She had worn it for Professor Hartley as soon as she had bought it and he had said that she reminded him of a character from a Brontë novel. When Alice had preened and asked – 'which character?' – he had said the *first* Mrs Rochester, the mad one in the attic.

That was Professor Hartley's idea of the perfect

joke. It demonstrated his knowledge (and that in a discipline other than his speciality), it squashed Alice's pretensions, and wounded her vanity. Thus it aided his control of Alice and established his superiority. In short, Professor Hartley was a bully and a clever dick.

Alice had taken off the dress and never worn it again. It had hung in her wardrobe for five years, waiting for a party where it might be excusable. Now, she realized, she could wear it every day if she wished. And no one, ever again, would wipe the smile off her face by telling her she looked ridiculous when she had thought she looked beautiful.

'You look beautiful,' Michael said tenderly.

Alice turned to him a face which was quite radiant.

They kissed like young lovers.

The aerobo-gardening class mowed and rolled the lawn to Dire Straits and started weeding the herbaceous borders with Madonna. Alice sat in the shade under the trees listening to the music and watching them with pleasure. She hardly turned her head when she heard the crunch of a heavy tread on the gravel and then a shadow fell on her.

'Oh! Doctor Simmonds!' she said. 'How nice to see you!'

Doctor Simmonds cast a jaundiced eye around the bright garden at the twenty skinny girls in sweat-stained leotards prancing long-legged behind the lawn-mower, or bending and hoeing in the flower beds, their bony bums bouncing to the beat.

'What's this?' he asked rudely. 'Bob-a-job?'

Alice privately thought that his diagnosis of death in an old lady who was merely drunkenly asleep could be easily explained if he seriously thought that the new Boy Scouts' uniform was a cut-away leotard with a boob-tube top.

'Yes,' she said, to avoid further explanations.

'Tell them they can come and do me next,' he said. He raised his voice to a stentorian shout: 'You can come and do me next!' he bellowed.

Stephanie jumped at the noise and then ran light-footed across the grass to Mrs Hartley. She had stripped down to a pair of footless tights which clung unreliably to her skinny hips. Her small apricot-shaped breasts bobbed sweetly under a cropped t-shirt top which occasionally slid off one shoulder to show an enticingly rosy nipple.

'You the Scout Captain?' Doctor Simmonds asked in some surprise.

Stephanie jogged from one thin foot to another in silence and looked to Mrs Hartley for guidance.

'Bit young to be Brown Owl, aren't you?' Doctor Simmonds demanded as the nipple hove into view and challenged his belief that Stephanie was a boy.

Stephanie did a few absent-minded scissor jumps. The t-shirt jumped too, revealing a tanned ribby midriff and the underside of her small pointy breasts.

'I said you can come and do me next,' Doctor Simmonds said. 'You look as if you could use some more work. I've got a hay meadow which needs cutting. A traditional hay meadow, I've got. I do it the old way – the real way – with a scythe. I love to be out in the open air with my scythe. You can all come behind me and stack.'

'Stack?' Alice asked, as if the verb were some obscene suggestion.

Doctor Simmonds glanced at her. 'Stack!' he said louder. 'It would do you the world of good, Madam, to get out into a hayfield, like my hayfield, and find out what real work is like.'

'Mrs Hartley,' Stephanie asked, hopping on one foot and then the other. 'Is this horrible man bothering you? Do you want me to disable him?'

Doctor Simmonds leaned forward as if he could not believe his ears. 'What? What? What did you say?' he demanded.

'It's all right, Stephanie,' Alice said sweetly. 'This is Doctor Simmonds, I can *certainly* handle him.'

Stephanie nodded and trotted away across the grass. Doctor Simmonds was purple with rage. The thought of being disabled by Stephanie was only marginally more insulting than being handled by Alice.

'Now look here,' he said. 'There are a few things I'd like to get straight. We'll go inside and sit down.'

He turned on his heel and marched firmly into the house. Alice, making wide aura-strengthening gestures with her hands, followed him, her blue embroidered gown hushing softly over the new-mown grass.

Doctor Simmonds was sitting at the kitchen table in the big carver chair. There was no sign of Aunty Sarah.

'I've heard some funny stories about this place,' he began truculently. 'And I expect an explanation.'

Alice hovered around to the other end of the table, still making aura-strengthening gestures. She hummed softly in her throat in praise of the Great Earth Mother whose service is simplicity and who, in happier, earlier and more straightforward times, would have ordered Doctor Simmonds's immediate ritual castration, disembowelment, and burning alive at the Midsummer Solstice.

'An explanation, d'you hear me?' said Doctor Simmonds more loudly. 'An explanation from you!'

Alice nodded and shimmered down into a seat. 'And what exactly is it that you don't understand?' she asked. 'Have you, perhaps, been asking yourself why your life seems so empty? Why you no longer desire your wife? Why you are bored, both with your work and with your hobbies? Are you worried about your excessive drinking and smoking, and the fact that you have no friends? Are you distressed that you are fat and ageing, balding, and unattractive, and that your breath smells and your clothes are ugly?' She smiled at him like a sibylline prophetess. 'Which of all these worries of yours – all of them, in their way, life-threatening – is uppermost in your mind?'

Doctor Simmonds burbled inarticulately – 'Why – how dare you?' he exploded. Spittle flew across the table in a shower of snow-white dots. 'How dare you, Mrs – Whatever-your-name-is?'

Alice smiled. 'You may call me Alice,' she said, as one conferring a boon on the humblest of suitors.

'I didn't come here to be insulted by you – you cheeky . . .' Doctor Simmonds cast around in his mind for the most insulting noun he could conjure. 'You cheeky . . . woman!' he said with loathing. 'I came here to find why you are pretending that old Miss Coulter is still alive! I came here to find out what sort of rum game you are playing, my lady! I came here to find what you're doing with a lad still wet behind the ears! *And* the district Scout Commissioner, who happens to be an old friend of mine, will be *very* interested in what you are doing with these Boy Scouts! Very interested indeed!'

'Then tell him,' Alice said encouragingly. She arose from her seat and went and opened the back door. Doctor Simmonds instinctively rose and followed her. Alice's flowery perfume, mixed with the scent of warm female sexuality, wafted over him and her gown brushed at his ankles.

'Tell him,' she said invitingly. 'And tell your wife that you made a mistake with Miss Coulter and that she is quite well, that she is better than she has ever been. And tell your wife, and the vicar's wife, that we are exploring consciousness here, that we are growing into unity with each other and with the whole universe.

'Tell them that the world is full of things which none of us understand, and that the key to deep joy is to watch and listen and learn. Not to pry and condemn.'

Doctor Simmonds gaped inarticulately.

'Tell them that it is possible to experience sexual pleasure so profoundly, and so deeply, that the sexual act is itself a way to consciousness. Have *you* ever made love which was so beautiful that you felt the presence of god all around you?' she asked. 'Have the two of you ever made love and wept for joy?'

Doctor Simmonds was grey with shock, but from his complacent fat-man's face a hungry little boy looked out. Alice saw the hunger in him, and knew how right she had been when she had teased him. He was bored, and lonely, and sick to his very soul.

'Oh, Doctor Simmonds,' she said with sudden pity. 'Come upstairs and get out of those ugly clothes and I will massage you all over with passion fruit and ginseng!'

For a moment he hovered, for a split second he swayed towards her; then he pushed himself back on his pompous heels and stormed out of the door.

'Soliciting, prostitution, and keeping a bawdy house!' he snarled. 'I have you now, Mrs Whoever-your-name-is! I have you now! You haven't heard the last of this by a long way. And the District Commissioner of Scouts will hear about this, *and* the parochial church council.'

'I don't doubt it,' Alice said sadly. She watched

him stomp off down the drive, muttering and threatening to himself as he went. She could hear him, like an ominous rumble of thunder on a sunny day, long after he had gone from her sight around the sweep of the drive.

She shut the back door and went and sat at the table and rested her head on her hands.

'Has he gone?' Aunty Sarah asked, emerging from the larder with an open bottle of elderflower champagne in her hand.

'Yes,' Alice said. 'What are you doing in there?'

'Hiding,' Aunty Sarah said precisely. 'And drinking.'

'Why?' Alice asked.

'I got bored waiting,' Aunty Sarah explained.

'Not the drinking, the hiding. Why are you hiding?'

Aunty Sarah leaned forward and breathed a warm boozy flower-scented breath into Alice's face. She tapped the side of her nose with one bony finger. 'He's going to be trouble, that one,' she said. 'Pity you couldn't get him upstairs and we could have taken photographs of him and threatened to put them on the church notice board unless he minded his own beeswax.'

Alice's eyes widened. 'That would be blackmail, Aunty Sarah!'

'They do it all the time on the radiovision,' Aunty Sarah said, unrepentantly. 'And I can tell you, that Constable Parkinson in the village is a nice enough little man, but Starsky and Butch he is not.'

'Too late now, anyway,' Alice said regretfully. 'And you are right, he is going to cause trouble if he can. What a pity he can't be made to see the opportunities of the world which is all around him. The mysteries!'

'Blind as a bat,' Aunty Sarah confirmed. 'He had a miracle healing before him – me – and he doesn't know it.'

'He could have a spacecraft land in his hayfield and he wouldn't see it,' Alice said mournfully. 'He is determined to see the worst and to cause disturbance and grief.'

'Not with me, he isn't,' Aunty Sarah said briskly. 'I'm not going back to bed to please anybody. I'm not going to be dead and buried either.'

Alice smiled. 'No, why should you!' she exclaimed. 'And I'm not going back to the Professor!'

Sarah poured two measures of the elderflower champagne into the breakfast teacups and they clinked them together in a mutual toast of defiance, and drank them to the dregs.

Aunty Sarah gleamed like a sadistic old lizard. 'I'll fix him,' she said. 'It's about time something happened to him.'

'Like what?' Alice said, immediately diverted.

'A spacecraft land in his hayfield,' Aunty Sarah said musingly. 'He's always been daft about that hayfield of his. Thinks he's the squire of the manor with it. He needs something to shake him up.'

When Michael returned from the university with

the Mothers and Babies it was in an unfamiliar car. Suzanne and Mary had brought a new recruit to the Growth Centre – Louise Biddings, hugely pregnant, was driving, wedged behind the steering-wheel of her pale blue Morris Minor. Suzanne sat in the front, Mary, Michael and the two babies were in the rear seat.

'Welcome,' Alice said warmly. She kissed them all in turn, breathing deeply when she turned her face into Michael's neck and all that warming testosterone wafted around her.

'This is Louise,' Suzanne said. 'She's married to a postgraduate research student in the politics department. She was due on Tuesday.'

Louise stood silent in her Jesus sandals, her eyes downcast, her dingy navy maternity smock billowing over her hugely pregnant belly.

'Hello,' Alice said pleasantly. 'Hello, Louise, come in and sit down.'

Louise waddled over the threshold and slumped on to the kitchen bench. Her hair was in lank rats' tails, she smelled warmly of old sweat and stale chip fat.

'I can't afford anything,' she said blankly. 'And he said I wasn't to come.'

'He?' Alice asked. She gestured to Michael to put the kettle on. Suzanne and Mary put their babies at either end of the pram and gave them a tea strainer and an ebony antique scarab to suck – redolent and tasty!

'Jon-Jo,' Louise said shortly. 'My husband. He

said that feminism and women's movements are false-consciousness splinter groups which threaten the hegemony of the revolution.'

'Oh,' Alice said.

'And I don't have any money since I gave up work in the chip shop.'

Alice nodded. She had not taken her eyes from Louise's sludge-coloured pudding face.

'When did you stop work?' she asked.

'On Tuesday,' Louise said. 'I got the sack, actually.'

Alice raised her eyebrows.

'My pains started,' Louise said. 'So I lay down behind the fryer. It's against Health and Safety Regs to block the fire exits. I was a Hazard,' she said with simple pride.

'Why doesn't your husband give you money?' Alice asked.

'He says property is theft,' Louise started. 'And he doesn't want me to be an enslaved dependant. I have to be free to negotiate my own level in the capitalist labour market – until the revolution, that is,' she said. She spoke of the coming revolution with resignation rather than with fervour.

Alice nodded. 'And what does he live on?' she asked.

'He's got a grant, and a scholarship, and money from his Dad,' Louise said without rancour. 'That's internal contradiction. He's taking money from the state and from the capitalists, and he uses it to overthrow the state and the capitalists. If he gave it to me it wouldn't be a revolutionary step. I don't do anything which is internal contradiction.'

'I see,' Alice said, who thought she saw all the most important things. 'And what about this baby?'

'We were an accident,' Louise said dully. 'And then he married me because my Dad's a miner.'

'He wanted to join the labouring classes by marrying you?' Alice asked.

Louise frowned, trying to remember. 'I think he said that,' she said. 'But the main reason was that my Dad said he'd break his bloody jaw.'

'And what does your doctor say about your pregnancy?' Alice asked.

Louise shrugged. 'He says "Next",' she said.

Alice nodded. 'Well then,' she said brightly. 'I understand that you cannot pay, Louise, but we can afford to let you have some treatment on credit, against the time when you *can* pay, how would that be?'

'All right,' Louise said. There was a glimmer of a smile on her tired face. 'That would be all right.'

'What I suggest you do first is go upstairs and have a hot bath and borrow one of my gowns,' Alice said. 'Michael will show you where to go, while I talk with Mary and Suzanne here.'

Michael poured the tea and put a mug for himself and Louise on the tray. Alice drew him to the far end of the kitchen.

'Get in the bath with her,' she said quietly.

Michael jumped. 'What? But she might not want me to!' he said.

'She will,' Alice said wisely. 'I shouldn't think he's laid a finger on her since he knocked her up. All Marxists are prudes. The only decent Marxists were wiped out with the Levellers. And don't tell me Tony Benn because if the Labour Party doesn't have the sense to pay any attention to him I don't see why I should!'

'No,' Michael said. 'I wasn't going to mention Tony Benn actually.'

Alice nodded. 'Wash her hair, and get her into my white nightgown, and a warm shawl, and then massage her back and her belly.'

Michael nodded obediently. 'I've never seen a pregnant woman all bare before,' he confided.

'That'll be nice for you, then,' Alice said generously. 'And Michael –'

'Yes?'

'When she wants to move rhythmically, encourage her. She needs to get that baby started.'

'Move? How should she move?' Michael asked, slightly confused.

'To a song, sing to her!' Alice said, smiling.

Michael had the tray in both hands, as Alice ushered him towards the stairs, Louise trailing, like an overloaded scow in his wake.

'What song?' he asked. 'I never sing!'

'Sing ten green bottles to her,' Alice said significantly. 'Ten green bottles, like you were singing to me, this morning.' She smiled at Michael's bewilderment and waved them off upstairs.

They took longer than Alice had expected; it was not until supper-time that they came down the stairs, hand-in-hand. Louise was wearing Alice's best nightgown, a long white Victorian gown with a high frilled neckline and exquisite pin-tucking in lines over her rounded breasts. Her hair was glossy and thick, waving down to her shoulders, framing her face which was round and pink-cheeked and glowing. Her eyes were very bright blue, and she was smiling.

'Hello, Louise!' Alice said warmly. 'Come and sit down and have some supper!'

Michael pulled out a chair for her, his hands rested on her shoulders as she sat.

Alice's clear swift scan took in Michael's tired smile and the weary slouch of his walk. 'Come here, darling,' she said and sat him beside her and put a bowl of mushroom soup before him. '*You* shall have some steak,' she said, nodding to Stephanie who was standing before the grill, an apron around her bare brown midriff. 'You will need your yang restoring.'

Michael nodded his thanks, Louise bent her head over the soup and ate hungrily. Alice watched her, smiling, and cut slices of home-made bread for them all. 'There,' she said with satisfaction. 'More herbal tea, Aunty Sarah?'

Aunty Sarah was resplendent in a gown of deep emerald green trimmed with peacock feathers sprouting from the neck, their patterns dancing like a thousand eyes. She was quite pissed.

'Thank you,' she said with quiet dignity. 'And a fruit extract chaser please, dear.'

Alice nodded and poured a peach brandy for her into the half-pint breakfast cup which Aunty Sarah preferred.

'How long have you lived here, Mrs Coulter?' Louise asked politely. 'It's a lovely house.'

Alice blinked. 'My name is Alice Hartley,' she said gently. 'Michael is my lover, not my husband.'

Louise's lips drooped into a wide gormless 'oo'. She put the back of her hand to her mouth. 'Oh no!' she said, dismayed. 'I thought he was your son, Mrs Hartley.'

Alice waved a small aura-strengthening gesture to ward off discomfort.

'No,' she said smoothly. 'Michael is my lover. We have lived together here for ages now.' She thought for a moment. 'Four days,' she said.

Louise looked aghast. 'I'm awfully sorry, Mrs Hartley,' she said. 'I didn't know. We were knocking it off upstairs together. I thought it was all right.'

163

There was silence at the supper table. Everyone was looking at Alice.

She smiled with effort. 'It was all right, Louise,' she said kindly. 'Your body needed that release, and Michael is a kind and generous lover. I expected him to make love with you. We do not have a mean and exclusive relationship. Michael and I share our love. We do not monopolize each other.'

Louise nodded, visibly unconvinced, stunned into silence.

Alice glanced down the table. 'We need more black pepper,' she said casually and went towards the large walk-in larder. She was gone for some minutes.

'And some more salt,' Michael said suddenly. He followed her into the larder.

She was leaning her forehead against the damp plaster of the outside wall.

'Are you all right?' he asked inadequately.

Alice opened her eyes. 'She's very young and very beautiful,' she said sadly. 'Very young.'

Michael shook his head vehemently. 'She's not!' he said.

Alice smiled sadly. 'I know she is,' she said. 'She's twenty years younger than me. She's the same age as you. Youth calls to youth I suppose.'

Michael shook his head again, fervently.

'It's *you* I want, Alice,' he said. 'It's *you* who is my lover. The rest is just growth.'

Alice looked at him with dawning hope in her face. 'Really?' she asked.

Michael struggled to find words which would tell Alice what she meant to him. 'Anyone can have a girlfriend,' he said. 'But you, Alice, you are a woman in your prime.'

The shadow lifted from Alice's face. She smiled. 'Yes,' she said. She moved forward, easily, into Michael's arms. He held her, kissed her lips, her closed eyelids, the soft surplus skin at the corner of her eyes. The lines at the corner of her mouth, tracks of her years of disappointment.

'I have been foolish,' Alice said. She nuzzled his warm firm neck. 'Forgive me, Michael.'

Michael patted her back. He felt magnanimous, in control. 'Silly girl,' he said lovingly. Alice let out a delighted giggle. 'Silly girl,' he said again. Arm in arm they returned to the supper table as Stephanie placed Michael's steak at his place.

Alice smiled all around and sliced more bread into generous, thick, inedible wodges.

'I say,' Louise said suddenly. 'I feel a bit funny.'

Alice looked at her sharply. 'Tell me how,' she commanded.

'I feel kind of faint,' Louise said. Suddenly she went pale and pitched forward on the table. 'Ooooh,' she said incredulously. 'Something moved.'

Alice nodded to Michael with a pleased smile.

Stephanie's eyes were as wide as saucers in her white face. 'Is she having it, Mrs Hartley?' she asked.

Gary, Jonafon and Timofy huddled together a little closer on the bench, two of the other aerobogardeners openly stared. Mary and Suzanne nodded wisely, like old hands.

'I should think so,' Alice said calmly.

Louise wailed. 'I've wet myself!' she said despairingly.

'That's your waters breaking,' Alice said. 'Just sit still, Louise, and let it happen. Your baby is coming.'

Jonafon went green, Timofy went white. Michael, who now knew more about pregnant women than many men *ever* know, calmly finished his steak with the air of a man who can see when a good job has been well done.

'Now where would you like your baby to be born?' Alice Hartley asked Louise, as if there were any option open to them but to telephone her husband and take her at once to the hospital.

Louise looked at Mrs Hartley with eyes suddenly widened by opportunity. 'Could I have it here?' she asked.

Mrs Hartley nodded. 'Of course,' she said.

'In the bath?' Louise asked wildly.

'A very good idea.'

Michael leaned towards Alice. 'Have you ever delivered a baby before?' he asked in an undertone.

'No,' Alice said. 'But I've seen it on television loads of times. And I know two obstetricians and *they* are thick as short planks. There can't be anything very complicated about it, you know, Michael.'

'No . . .' Michael said, unconvinced.

Alice smiled and patted his hand. 'Trust to Nature, Michael,' she said. 'Louise needs to get in touch with deep elemental forces.' She paused thoughtfully. 'I don't think the bathroom is quite elemental enough,' she said. 'What we really want is the sea! And a school of dolphins!'

'There's the dolphinarium, down at the sea-front,' Stephanie offered. 'If you want dolphins, Mrs Hartley, they've got four there. They're called Bilbo and Bibby and Peety and Tutu.'

'Dolphins?' Alice exclaimed. She turned quickly to Louise. 'Dear Louise, wouldn't you like to give birth in touch with the deepest elemental forces? Wouldn't you like to give birth to your baby with dolphins playing all around you?'

Louise's blue eyes widened. 'Could we do that?' she asked.

Alice threw her arms wide and her blue sleeves billowed. 'Why not?' she demanded. 'All things are possible for people who are prepared to take risks to seek their heart's desire. *Is* it your heart's desire to give birth with dolphins?'

Louise gave a little squeak of agreement and then a louder squeak as a contraction gripped her.

'Come then!' Alice said grandly. 'Come! We shall need some helpers. Aunty Sarah, you stay here and look after the babies. Suzanne and Mary, you come with us. Gary and Timothy and Jonathon and Stephanie, you follow in your car. Michael, you help Louise into our car and then bring some towels and blankets.'

She paused for thought for a moment. 'And rainbow trout,' she said. 'I've got some in the freezer. Better bring them too!' Alice was hazy as to whether dolphins were total abstainers from meat, but in the dark, in a pool with a new-born baby, she thought they would be wise to take no chances.

The Sargent Oceanside Marine Park was a grim little acreage set at the west end of the promenade where the handsome Regency buildings deteriorated into Victorian copies and then into Edwardian tat. Alice had never been near it, regarding such places as blots on the face of the Great Earth Mother. With Michael directing her, she drove carefully up to the main gate which was chained and padlocked. In the watchman's hut the flickering blue of a small portable television screen indicated that security was lax. The booming voice of the television quiz-master – unchallenged by any shouted guess at the questions from the watchman – indicated that he was stupid as well as deaf.

Alice left the car purring in neutral and she and Michael approached the gate armed with wire cutters. Ignoring the padlock and chain altogether, they cut a car-shaped outline from the wire mesh and carefully bent it back. Alice drove the car softly through the hole, Gary, Timofy, Jonafon and Stephanie followed in Gary's Mini, and then Michael peeled the wire mesh back into place.

'The dolphins are straight ahead,' Suzanne said from the back seat, where she and Mary were cradling Louise's contented bulk in their arms.

Alice clicked the car into gear and, lit only by pale starlight, moved forward to the pool where the dolphins performed their tricks at hourly intervals during the season. There was a ramp at the rear of the pool to aid the delivery of fresh dolphins when the veterans had died of heartbreak and boredom, and Alice turned Professor Hartley's Jaguar and backed it up the ramp to the very rim of the pool.

Louise stood at the water's edge, shivering slightly in the evening air. Every now and then she would grunt as a contraction clamped on her stomach. Alice noticed the grunts were getting closer together and more urgent. Michael draped a blanket around Louise's shoulders and Mary and Suzanne held both her hands and walked her around the perimeter of the pool.

'Dolphins!' Alice called out over the dark lapping waters. 'Dolphins, where are you?'

There was no answer.

'P'raps they sleep in a different pool?' Stephanie suggested.

'I didn't think they did sleep,' Michael said.

'Everyone sleeps sometime, man,' Gary offered.

'Ssh,' Alice said. 'I am communicating with them.'

They all fell obediently silent. Louise, walking on the rim of the pool in her white nightgown, every now and then stopping and saying 'unnhh', was like an initiate in some ancient rite. Alice, with her arms outstretched, her blue gown billowing in the night air, and the star and moon embroidery sparkling in the starlight, was chief priestess.

'Dolphins!' she called again.

'Bilbo!' Stephanie called. 'Bibby! Peety! Tutu!'

'Dolphins!' Alice called.

There was a wonderful crackle of noise, and three, and then four smooth snouts appeared from nowhere, and lay on the rim of the pool at Alice's bare feet.

'Oh Dolphins!' she said in delight. 'Here – have a libation.'

She reached out a hand to Michael who solemnly handed her the rainbow trout bag. She gave each dolphin a rainbow trout and they each snapped it up and then walked backwards on their tails, waving their flippers and singing in their grunting crackling noises, then they all simultaneously somersaulted and raced around the pool to end up, nose-by-nose, at Alice's feet again.

'No, no,' said Alice, rather disapproving. 'That's not the kind of thing that's wanted at all.'

She bent down to them and stroked their smooth snouts and felt their wet sides. 'Don't,' she said gently. 'Don't do any of that stupid stuff now. This is serious. I want you to act like dolphins, not performing seals.'

One dolphin whistled softly through his blowhole. 'A bit of dignity!' Alice urged. 'A bit of dignity and get in touch with your real selves!'

The dolphins were silent, perhaps they felt reproved.

Alice straightened up.

'I think it's coming!' Mary called urgently from the other side of the pool.

Alice stepped forward, the moon escaped from a net of clouds and shone dimly as Alice took the hem of her blue gown in both hands and drew it up over her head. Beneath her gown she was completely naked. Her large white body gleamed in the half-light like some heroic statue mythically aroused.

'Come,' she commanded. 'All of you! Naked into the pool!'

'Gosh,' said Michael. Then he and Gary and Timofy and Jonafon, Mary, Suzanne and Louise stripped off their clothes and slid into the dolphins' soupy water.

To the dolphins, this was something of a novelty. Their trainer – a dour Mancunian by the name of George Mells – usually commanded them with a referee's whistle from the side and preferred not to get wet. He had had trouble with his adenoids until the age of eighteen and never learned to swim. For the grand finale of the act his current girlfriend was persuaded to come out in a skimpy bikini, get into the water, and be towed around the pool by one of the dolphins. She did this with such reluctance and with such a bad grace that the dolphins sensed her sulkiness and tried again and again to cheer her by dipping her under water, or playfully wriggling out of her grip leaving her sinking in the deep end. They were always hurt and a little disappointed that she never seemed to be cheered at all.

So it was rather a surprise and a delight to them to feel the quivers in the water as happy naked young people kicked and splashed. The dolphins cruised cautiously among the swimmers, and then one (possibly Peety), a little more daring than the rest, slid between Alice Hartley's white thighs and gave her a ride around the pool.

Alice screamed with surprise, and the joy of exploring yet another sensation which Professor Hartley had been temperamentally and physically incapable of providing. Then Michael grabbed a strong fin as it went past him and was dragged through the water too. Soon they were all rollicking and splashing and playing and the undiscriminating moonlight showed a shadowed curve of buttock and smooth grey back of equal beauty.

'Alice!' Louise called. 'I think something's happening!'

Alice, recalled to her principal role, swam over to Louise and held her around the shoulders.

'Breathe deeply,' she said. 'Your baby is embarking on his or her first great journey and adventure. She or he is full of wonder and joy. She or he is going to come from the warm waters of your body into the warm waters of the pool and be greeted with elemental forces, water, moonlight, dolphins, your new friends, and your smile.'

Louise nodded. Her face was sweating and every now and then she made a deep satisfying groan. Michael held one of her hands, Suzanne the other. Stephanie, like a little dolphin herself, trod water at Louise's feet and eyed her pubic hair – swaying in the water like a clump of seaweed – with deep suspicion and reserve.

'Gently,' Alice Hartley crooned. A dolphin swam speedily underneath them and the whole group bobbed with the passing wave. '*Give* birth,' Alice Hartley murmured. 'You don't force birth, or take birth. You *give* birth. Be gentle with yourself, Louise.'

Louise started breathing more quickly. Alice looked around. Gary, Timofy and Jonafon were clinging to the side of the pool behind her with their arms around each other's thin necks. Mary and Stephanie were each holding Louise's feet.

'Gary, Timothy and Jonathon, come closer,' Alice said lovingly. 'Come and be ready to greet your little brother or sister. Gary, hold Louise's thigh. You too, Timothy. Jonathon, be ready to help the dolphins raise the baby up to the air.'

Alice had every trust in the elemental forces of nature but she could not help but have doubts about animals who answered to names such as Peety, Bilbo, Tutu and Bibby. And she had been disappointed by their readiness to perform foolish and undignified stunts.

Louise gave a convulsive heave and a shriek.

'What can you see, Jonathon?' Alice asked.

Jonafon was goggle-eyed. He had never seen a cunt before in his life. Now he was expected to stare at one – and as he looked it opened up like some terrifying flower and, clearly, he could see the dark mat of a tiny head.

'I can see a head!' he gulped.

'Gently then, gently,' Alice instructed.

Louise heaved for air and floated trustingly on the water, supported by gentle hands. Her stomach rose, went rigid, and as she groaned Jonafon gave a yelp of amazement as the baby slithered out. He stretched out his hands to catch it, but the baby was wet and slippery, and Jonafon was nervous.

'Oh damn!' he said in exasperation. 'I've dropped it, Mrs Hartley!'

'Well, pick it up,' Alice said, exhaling deeply to keep her irritation from invading her aura. 'Pick it up, Jonathon darling.'

The moon went back behind the clouds and darkness enveloped the pool. Alice could see nothing but she could hear Jonafon floundering around.

'I can't find it,' he said desperately. 'It's floating around somewhere. I had it in my hands and now it's slithered out and sunk somewhere.'

'My baby!' Louise called anxiously.

'It's down here somewhere,' Jonafon said helpfully.

Alice could see nothing in the murky waters; the moonlight came and went, never bright enough to illuminate the darkness of the deep water. Alice gritted her teeth in fear.

'Can anyone dive?' she asked. 'Can anyone go underwater and find the baby?'

She looked around. All the faces were white and aghast. No one was competent to cope with this emergency. They were all looking to her, and Alice did not know what to do. A deep fast wave bulged underneath them. The group bobbed on the turbulent water, Alice experienced rising panic as a swiftly moving swell of the water hit them and a dolphin beneath them brushed against her legs, nosing around where the baby had sunk.

'Where's the baby?' she said urgently. 'Jonathon – feel below you for the cord. We must get the baby up to the air at once!'

As she spoke, Bibby the dolphin nosed up out of the waters of the deep end. Before him, as pale and perfect in the starlight as a floating cowrie shell, he pushed the baby with his long gentle nose.

'The dolphin brought it,' Alice said incredulously. 'The dolphin brought it up!'

Louise held out her arms and the dolphin gently nosed the floating baby towards her. The baby was on his back, his eyes open and as he saw the sky, he took his first breath of air, and he cooed, a trusting sound of joy. Louise let out a little cry of wonder, and held him to her, and the dolphin laid his long beaky nose on her shoulder, wearing the asinine grin of a proud father.

'A boy,' Alice said with delight.

'I want to name him after the dolphins,' Louise said with sudden determination. 'This has been the most wonderful moment of my life. I want to name him after the dolphins, all four names. What are they, Alice?'

Alice shut her eyes for a brief moment, thinking of what life would be like for little Bilbo Bibby Peety Tutu Biddings on his first day at school.

'Their proper name,' she said, 'their Latin name,

is Daniel. You shouldn't name your son after nick-names. Call him Daniel which means dolphin.'

Michael leaned over and kissed Alice's bare shoulder in the water. 'You know so much,' he said respectfully.

Alice glowed. She knew she did. Knowing some-thing from your imagination is equal in merit to knowing it because you happened to read it in a book written by some dried-up old idiot of a pro-fessor.

'Now,' she said. 'Let's get Louise and Daniel home to bed.'

Louise suddenly clutched her hand. 'No!' she said. 'I don't want to go home! I don't want Daniel to be a worker for the cause, I don't want him to be a foot soldier in the remorseless army of revolu-tion.'

Alice patted her reassuringly, and heaved herself out of the pool. 'Certainly not,' she said. Jonafon, Timofy and Gary boosted Louise from behind while Michael and Alice pulled from in front. Gary, for the first time in his life, felt the compact rounded buttocks of a woman in both his hands – and discov-ered, to his awestruck amazement, that he liked it.

'You are coming home with us!' Alice said joy-fully. 'And Daniel is not going to be a soldier in the revolution. He is going to be a wholly integrated person!'

'Oh good,' Louise said.

Alice towelled herself briskly dry and stepped back into her blue gown. Gary, who had grown a good deal in personal sexual terms in the past ten minutes, watched the disappearance of Alice's bushy pubic hair and broad white hips with regret.

Alice walked back to the rim of the pool.

'Daniels, we are grateful to you,' she said. Her voice was clear and sweet over the dark moving waters. 'And we acknowledge that you have helped us. I am waiting for a sign from you if there is anything you want from us?'

Alice stood very still and held her mind in quiet readiness. She waited for mental images of a pint of prawns, say; or a box of mackerel. But she saw nothing.

At least, all she saw was the image printed on her retina of a light sky and darker water.

'Oh,' she said, rather surprised.

'What do they want?' Michael asked rather anxiously. He knew these dolphins had been doing tricks at the end of the pier for a long, long time. He was aware they would have seen many desirable consumer goods during that time, especially cameras. He had a small private fear that they would want a state-of-the-art rapid-focus and automatic rewind camera, or a video camcorder; and he was afraid for his Nikon camera which his mother had given him last birthday. If the dolphins wanted it, he was sure that Alice would make him give it to them.

Alice recovered from her surprise and beamed at him. 'They want to be free,' she said simply. 'They want to be in the sea.'

'Oh yes,' Michael said. He was so relieved about the Nikon that the implications of what Alice said did not sink in.

'What?' he asked. Then, 'But, Alice, we can't set them free!'

Alice rounded on him, her dark eyes flashing. 'Why not?'

'Because they belong to someone,' Michael said feebly. 'Someone bought them.'

'All property is theft,' Louise murmured out of habit, while Mary and Suzanne wrapped her warmly in blankets.

'Exactly,' Alice said brightly. 'You can't own a person can you?'

'Well, no,' Michael said. 'Slavery is illegal.'

'And these are people aren't they?' Alice asked.

'Well, they're dolphins,' Michael offered.

'Have they proved their humanity tonight?' Alice demanded.

Michael nodded; the memory of Bibby, the dolphin's broad shiny grin as he pushed the baby towards Louise, was very vivid.

'Then they are people. And we pay our debts,' Alice said sternly.

Michael shrugged. 'But how do we get them to the sea?' he asked.

Alice looked around. The walls around the pool were steep, the sea washed invitingly on the other side – but there was a long shingle beach to the first wavelets.

'We'll have to drive them,' she said.

Michael had a picture of himself herding squirming dolphins seawards, a lariat looped casually around his wrist, a Marlboro cigarette drooping casually out of the corner of his mouth.

'In the car,' Alice said.

In moments she had reorganized the cars. Gary drove Mary, Suzanne, Louise and baby Daniel home to the Growth Centre, while Jonafon, Timofy and Stephanie waited behind with Michael and Alice to pay their debts to the Daniels.

Alice patted the water with her hand. 'Come on dolphins,' she called. Almost at once a firm rounded snout pressed into her palm. Alice nodded to Michael and the two boys, who obediently stripped off again and slid into the water. The dolphin grinned cooperatively and lay still as they knotted an improvised sling of Jonafon and Timofy's matching pale blue dungarees beneath its creamy grey belly.

Alice held its head while they heaved it out of the pool and on to the side.

'Now what?' Michael asked, panting.

'Into the car,' Alice said. She stepped back to avoid getting wet and slipped her dress off again and spread it out carefully over one of the seats at the poolside. 'Gently now,' she said.

Reverently they laid the dolphin on the smooth leather back seat of Professor Hartley's one-time concourse-condition Jaguar car.

'I'll stay here and pour water over it while you get the other one,' Alice said. She leaned over the dolphin and wrung little streams of water out of her thick hair. The dolphin clicked agreeably, enjoying the smell of the walnut dashboard and high-octane fuel, and the feel of hand-stitched leather upholstery.

Michael, Jonafon, Timofy and Stephanie heaved the second dolphin on to the floor in the back of the car.

'Will he be all right?' Michael asked.

'Wet those dungarees and spread them over him,' Alice said. 'It's only a short way.'

They drove out carefully past the watchman's hut. A long whine from the television indicated that the station had closed down, and the watchman had closed down also. Now and then there was a rumbling snore from one of them.

Alice drove through the hole in the mesh and turned to the right along the promenade. The big car slid easily through the moonlight, passing piles of chained deck-chairs and a white-painted shelter with seats. A little way along there was a ramp for towing boats out of the sea. Alice drove past it and then reversed the car down with ill-founded confidence.

She left the motor running and helped the boys and Stephanie unload the two dolphins.

'We won't take them out deep straight away,' she said. 'We'll let them all go together.'

They gently laid the two dolphins in the shallows where the waves could wash over them. They clicked and whistled companionably, apparently content to wait and see what would happen next. So far, it seemed to have nothing to do with hoops, balls, trumpets or funny hats, which was a relief in itself.

Alice made the return journey and supervised the loading of the last two dolphins. She folded her dress and put it in the boot, not wanting to get it wet. Then she drove carefully towards the hole in the wire mesh again.

The watchman, awake at last, heard the purr of the well-tuned engine and stumbled out of his hut, flashing his torch wildly around. He saw the Jaguar-shaped hole in the mesh and let out a bellow of rage.

'Who did this then?' he demanded of the silent sky. Then he wheeled around and saw the silver-grey Jaguar coming slowly towards him.

The British class system is a great and potent power. As soon as he saw the expensive elegance of the car he put a finger to his cap and stepped to one side. Alice regally bowed her head and impercept-ibly pressed the accelerator.

As the great car gathered speed and swept past him, the watchman could see that the driver was a woman and her passengers were three young men and one girl, all of them completely naked. And in the back, one on the floor of the car and one on the seat, wearing matching pale blue denim dungarees, were two dolphins.

'Stop!' he shouted. But it was too late. Alice and the Daniels were gone.

'We'll have to be quick,' she said as she parked

the car at the foot of the ramp. 'He'll probably call the police.'

Jonafon, Stephanie, Timofy and Michael hastily heaved the two dolphins from the car to the shallows. All four lay along the beach, like great idle lubbery trippers with a day-return ticket from Manchester.

'We'll have to help them out to sea,' Alice said.

They waded into the water. It was surprisingly warm. The shingle underfoot sucked and seethed, the little pebbles tickling, teasing. The tide was coming in. As the waves washed in deeper and deeper, they heaved on tail fluke and fin to shift the dolphins to deeper water. The dolphins wiggled helpfully, grinned around at them, crackled and clicked. Waist-deep in foaming water they each took a dolphin and urged it outwards, away from the land, away from Sargent's Oceanside Marine Park, away from the frozen coley and the balls and the depressed girl in the bikini. And each dolphin, tasting authentic salt water for the first time in a long while, rose up to the surface, pointing its long conical snout at the yellow moon, and blew out and gurgled to each other in delight, and chuckled and remembered long swims from ocean to ocean, and told dirty jokes and sang comic songs about moonlight on the water and female dolphins, and the chummy pleasures of spawning grounds.

Alice and Michael and Stephanie and Jonafon and Timofy swam alongside them, further and further out to sea into deeper and deeper water as the broad butter moon sank slowly down in the west and the dark sky overhead became lighter grey, and then pink with the rising sun.

Then, when the dolphins were safely out in deep water, and heading southerly, Alice stroked their smooth flanks and told them farewell. They circled her, and the four others, as if to share the freedom of the seas together. Then, with their broad tails beating deeply and silently in the dark currents, the four headed south to the ocean, and the others headed north to the land.

They never saw each other again.

But none of them ever forgot.

MONDAY MORNING

At home, in the early hours of the day, Michael and
Alice melted into one another's arms and slept the
sleep of innocent children. They were drained of
desire by their earlier satisfaction, they had been
physically stretched by heaving the dolphins in and
out of the car, they were emotionally sated by the
joy of childbirth, and they were knackered. Once
Michael stirred, and cuddled a little closer to Alice's
broad back, Blinkie questing for a home in the
warm darkness of the bedclothes. Alice, still completely asleep, put a strong white hand behind her
and clamped Michael's penis between the welcoming damp warmth of her thighs with practised ease.
Michael slept again.

In the morning he was fresh and joyous but Alice
was weary.

'You look tired,' Michael said.

'Not at all,' Alice said, grouchy. She felt old.

'Shall I bring you a cup of tea in bed?' he offered.
'I'm going in for an early lecture. Gary and Jonafon
and Timofy are taking me.'

Alice nodded. For a brief contradictory moment she longed for Professor Hartley's sullen unbreakable silence before 10 a.m. and the middle-aged settled routine of her old home.

'All right,' she said ungraciously.

Michael pattered barefoot out of the room, and came back a few moments later with a cup of tea and a copy of the *Guardian*.

'There,' he said. 'Now you can be comfy.'

Alice glanced at the headlines. The government were going to axe all the remaining grants which had been accidentally left available from the last round of cuts, and give the money thus saved to the extremely rich – this is called incentive. Someone had taken a photograph of Princess Diana dancing with a strange man in a nightclub which was held to prove how strong the royal marriage now is (though it *did* go through a sticky period a little while ago). There was a military coup on an island in the Pacific which no one had ever heard of. One of the newly privatized companies – Gas, Water, Electricity, or Telephones – was poisoning, or cheating, or robbing its helpless customers. The consumer agency specifically established to prevent this abuse of power was surprised and baffled to find it had no control over this loophole, no legal status, and no punitive powers. Another Arab splinter group had decided to join in whatever trouble was currently raging in the Middle East, justifying their expenditure and death rate by their glorious history – unknown till now. An American woman was taking a man to court for an offence against her which she had richly deserved, or for which there could be no excuse, depending on the reader's preconceptions of the nature of womanhood (see interminable editorial).

There were riots and uprisings in an unpronounceable place in what used to be the USSR. There was a famine in central Africa, Hartlepool had been relegated off the bottom of the league table to outer darkness. Peace talks in Northern Ireland had broken down but hopes remained high of a settlement sometime within the next millennium. Hemlines would be longer this autumn, except for those which would be dramatically short.

'That's nice isn't it?' Michael said encouragingly.

Alice looked at him. Behind his round-rimmed glasses his eyes glowed with stupidity and affection, like a well-trained inbred puppy. 'That'll cheer you up,' he said.

'Yes,' Alice said gloomily. 'Thank you, darling. This will cheer me up a lot.'

Michael bent over and gave her a swift kiss. 'I'll be back at lunchtime,' he said. 'Gary, Jonathon and Timothy want to come out this afternoon as well. They'll bring me home. They're going to buy a cot for Daniel.'

Alice nodded and waved Michael out of the room, then she drank her tea, carefully avoiding even glancing at one word of the miseries of the world, drew herself a bath, and prescribed an extended floating meditation with fruit extract supplements. In other words, Alice retreated to the bathroom with a bottle of sloe gin and did not come out until she felt better.

She took three hours but by eleven o'clock, dressed in a long sweeping red gown and swathed in gold and black scarves, Alice drifted drunkenly down the stairs to be greeted with the surprising vision of Aunty Sarah, swathed from head to toe in virginal white, giving an interview to half a dozen reporters and three photographers who were gathered respectfully on the front steps.

'These alien life forces have been naturally drawn to the doctor,' Aunty Sarah proclaimed. 'He is a great believer in these kinds of things. I am not at all surprised that they chose his hayfield to land on.'

'Aunty Sarah, what is this?' Alice asked, coming forward.

Sarah turned, her face luminous with innocent candour. 'Such exciting news!' she said. 'They've found crop circles in Doctor Simmonds's hay, in his hayfield.'

'Really?' Alice exclaimed. She brushed past the journalists and walked down the drive, and crossed the road to the hayfield which ran the length of the road alongside the doctor's house. Today all the curtains in the Simmonds' house were drawn tight against the invasion of the public, they did not even twitch. A scramble of cars was parked crookedly on the verge of the road, blocking access to Rithering village. Twenty or thirty people were trampling down the hay in Doctor Simmonds's precious meadow, walking up and down, admiring the wide flat circle which had appeared, as if by magic, in the very centre of the meadow.

Alice breathed in a deep sigh of excitement and pleasure. She walked through the gap in the hedge where the broken fence posts marked the excessive enthusiasm of the man from the *Sun* newspaper, and strode towards the circle. It was about twenty feet across. A wide green circle, with the fresh green hay squashed symmetrically down in a perfect pattern.

Alice took her crystal on its chain from around her neck and held it carefully in one hand.

'Are you communicating with me?' she asked the indifferent air and the sunny morning. 'Have you come here to give me a sign?'

The crystal moved slightly in the warm breeze. Alice glanced around the field. There were hordes of nutters and charlatans trying to dowse with sticks or with crystals on string, or with Y brackets of wire. Alice sighed impatiently. All these amateur dabblers would interrupt her communication with the powers which were coming through. She could feel the free flow of her communication to other astral planes being blocked by their slap-happy amateurism.

'Are you getting through?' a little weasel-faced man at her elbow asked. 'Who d'you think did it, Missus?'

Alice spread her arms wide. The sleeves of the

red gown billowed dramatically. There was a rattle of sound behind her as a dozen camera shutters whirred and clicked. Alice affected not to notice.

'I feel another life force,' she said. 'I feel it very powerfully.'

'Was it pranksters?' the man asked. 'Practical jokers?'

Alice glanced at him and turned away. 'It may be powers from another astral plane,' she said thoughtfully. 'Or powers from another planet. Or, who knows, it may be my own psychic power which is manifesting itself in Doctor Simmonds's hay –' she paused. 'I am surprised it happened in Doctor Simmonds's meadow. I would not have thought him the sort of man to attract psychic energy.'

'He won't speak to us,' the reporter offered resentfully. 'What sort of a man is he?'

'Lumpish,' Alice said graphically. 'Stupid. All sorts of miracles have occurred around him all his life and he denies them. Miracle cures, crop circles, growth, natural birth, he denies everything.'

The reporter was writing frantically. 'And it always happens around him?' he asked.

'Of course,' Alice said gently. She was barely listening to him. 'His life, like that of everyone on this planet, is a whirlwind of powerful phenomena. But he pretends that none of it takes place. He pretends that nothing happens.'

'That'll do for me!' the reporter said, pleased. 'I'll be off now.' He nodded at Alice and scuttled off through the field, waving his arms at a mobile film unit who were unpacking at the corner of the hay meadow. Alice barely noticed he had gone. She was attuning to the energy of the crop circle and before her half-shut eyes she could see, with mysterious clarity, eight or even twelve moving shapes. Probably UFOs, possibly parent-ships. Undoubtedly trying to communicate with her.

Alice spent some time in the hayfield. She only left when the Rithering local policeman came and ordered everyone out, warning them of the laws against trespass and damage, and tied a strip of white and red plastic across the gap in the hedge. As the field emptied of psychic day-trippers Alice saw the kitchen curtain twitch as Mrs Simmonds regarded the trampled wasteland of what had been her husband's pride and joy, his hobby hayfield, his little bit of rural England.

Alice drifted home, her head full of strange incomplete sentences and a throbbing ache, communications, no doubt, from Beyond.

Aunty Sarah was in the sitting-room, she beckoned Alice in. 'Come and see this! Come and see this!' she exclaimed delightedly.

It was the midday local news on the television. The first shot was an aerial inspection of the Simmonds' paddock. As the helicopter hovered you could see the Simmonds' back door open and Patricia Simmonds come out into the garden, holding her iron-grey permed curls with both hands and staring upwards at the noise. Then the down-blast of the helicopter engine snatched at her washing line and one end broke free. With one hand still on her hair, Patricia Simmonds tried to catch the wildly flapping line and rescue her washing. Watched by all the viewers of the South Television area, Patricia Simmonds struggled to hold her laundry down to earth. All over the home counties hundreds of bored women watching midday television and drinking the cooking sherry sniggered in malicious joy as one week's wash billowed up, up, and finally tore free of its moorings and vanished out of sight.

'Watch!' Aunty Sarah commanded.

The reporter who had been in the field with Alice was now beaming out of the television screen.

'Today as I stood at the edge of the latest crop circle phenomenon in the little village of Rithering, local people told me that the owner of this field, Doctor James Simmonds, lives among a vortex of paranormal happenings. This is not the first time that extraordinary events have happened around him. His neighbours tell of miracle births, faith healing and extraordinary cures, which are putting the village of Rithering on the map as the psychic centre of the south.'

The film cut rapidly to a picture of the Simmonds' doorway half open and Doctor Simmonds's face, purple with rage, peering around the crack of the door and mouthing obscenities.

'The doctor denies his extra-normal powers,' the reporter went on, 'possibly for fear that his talents might be abused. But his neighbours, who have just launched an Alternative Healing and Growth Centre, attest to his living in what they call a whirlwind of unexplained phenomena.'

The film cut back to the little man in front of the field. Behind him in the background, among the other dowsers and believers, was Alice holding out her crystal and waiting for a message.

'Whatever the cause, the local doctor of Rithering woke up this morning to find himself a media sensation!' the reporter proclaimed. 'And students of the paranormal will be beating a path to his house at Rithering for a long time to come!'

In case any nutter had any doubt where to find the doctor, the film ended with a long panned shot of the main road into Rithering and focused on his house. The report ended. The bland face and aggressive hair of the midday newsreader replaced the picture of Rithering, and her perky, falsely bright voice started hammering the guts out of another non-story. Alice clicked the switch off.

'Doctor Simmonds isn't going to like that,' Alice said thoughtfully.

Sarah nodded her head in complete agreement. She looked like a satisfied boa constrictor which has just swallowed a hugely enjoyable pig belonging to someone else.

'I think I'll have a little lie down,' she said. 'I'm exhausted with all this excitement. Fancy Doctor Simmonds being the centre of miraculous phenomena and alien spacecraft landings.'

Alice glanced at Sarah, her suspicions alerted.

'Aunty Sarah,' she said. 'It wasn't anything to do with you, was it?'

Sarah leaned forward and patted Alice's hand. 'Doesn't matter, does it?' she asked sweetly. 'Just as long as Simmonds has something else to worry about and keeps his nose out of our business?'

Alice gasped. '*You* did the crop circle?' she demanded.

Sarah nodded. 'Last night,' she said with quiet satisfaction. 'While I was baby-sitting. You said Simmonds wouldn't believe a spacecraft if it landed in his own hayfield. So I did it! Now we'll see what he makes of that! And it'll keep him too busy to come in upsetting us while we are doing so nicely. Keep him out of our hair for a while, won't it?'

Alice felt herself smiling. 'You did it?' she confirmed.

Aunty Sarah nodded, her lizard-bright eyes gleaming. 'I've settled him,' she said. 'He won't be coming over here bothering us. He won't be seen dead on our doorstep in case someone thinks he's converted! And he can moan all he likes to the parish council – no one's going to listen to him when they've said on the radiovision that he's a crank.'

Alice took Aunty Sarah's hands. 'You are a spiteful and scheming old lady,' she said. 'And I love you very much. That was an inspired thing to do. The vicar is on our side, the doctor is discredited. We're home and dry. Nothing can hurt us now!'

But even as she spoke, you – the reader – felt a deep sense of foreboding. For you are aware of the convention of Dramatic Irony, even if Alice is not. This is the device whereby just as everyone says that everything is wonderful ... something goes dreadfully wrong. And Alice said the worst thing that anyone in a novel ever can say.

Why do they never learn – these fictional characters who so blithely trigger their own dénouement? They read enough novels – we see them reading all the time. Some of them, indeed, tediously many of them, are novelists. Why, therefore, do they not realize that it is Utterly Fatal to express any satisfaction with life in a novel? Better by far to moan on like Silas Marner than to dance like Polyanna towards a zimmer frame.

'We're home and dry,' Alice said with satisfaction.

The reader gasped.

There was a thunderous knock at the front door.

Alice strolled across the hall, the heels of her sandals tapping on the loose tiles and opened half of the big double door. It was Doctor Simmonds on the doorstep, not at all abashed at his sudden rise to fame, angrier, fatter and even redder-faced than yesterday.

For one brief childishly hopeful moment, Alice thought that he might have been so shocked by the dramatic communication from Aliens (or Aunty Sarah) that he had come to be stripped naked and rubbed all over with passion fruit and ginseng; but then she saw his scowling face and knew he had come for a very different satisfaction. He had come to get back at Alice for telling him that he was fat and old and ugly.

Also, without evidence to support him, he blamed her for the crop circle and for his sudden reputation as the guru of Rithering. He did not need to know about Synchronicity to believe that Alice Hartley meant trouble for conventionally minded stick-in-the-muds like himself. And he believed that everything which had gone wrong since Alice had arrived in the village was somehow connected with her.

And there was worse.

With Doctor Simmonds, standing half a pace behind him with an expression of studied neutrality, was a man she did not know. He was wearing an ill-cut suit, shiny at the seams. It was a suit which was trying so hard to look like a suit which a normal person might choose off a rack with the exercise of his free will, that Alice knew at once, with a sinking heart, that he must be a CID officer trying to look like a normal man in a normal suit.

He took the lead. 'Inspector Bromley, Brighton CID,' he said, a man too important to waste time with verbs. 'Can we come in, Missus?' He was half-way across the doorstep before Alice murmured, 'Yes,' and led the way into the dining-room. Out of the corner of her eye Alice saw Aunty Sarah drift noiselessly and unseen up the stairs to avoid Doctor Simmonds once again.

Alice seated herself in the large carver chair behind the massive dining-table with the wide bow window behind her. She let them perch themselves dangerously on Professor Hartley's stacking studio chairs which creaked and tipped warningly when they moved too quick.

Alice moved a sheet of clean paper before her and picked up a pen. Her hands were trembling slightly but she felt better with the artefacts of Professor Hartley's power around her.

'How can I help you?' she asked.

'Firstly, let's have some details,' the CID man said. 'You are?'

Alice told him her name and former address and he wrote it down very carefully, checking the spelling of everything. When he came to her surname he turned back his notebook to a marked place and compared the spelling against something already written on an earlier page. Alice felt her throat tighten with anxiety. She was wondering if he had come about the Jaguar.

'Date of birth?' the policeman asked.

Alice told him.

'That means, you are now . . .' he paused while he completed slow but essential mental arithmetic. Alice tried to be amused by the delay but it seemed to her that he deliberately took an unflattering length of time, as if he were working through the twenties and the thirties and thinking about taking his socks off to use his toes to help him count through the forties and fifties.

'I'm forty-two,' she said snappishly at the very moment when he had worked it out for himself.

'As I thought,' the Inspector said, with conspicuous lack of gallantry. 'And do you live here, Mrs Hartley? Is this your permanent address?'

Alice nodded. The doctor shifted impatiently in his seat and muttered, 'Hardly permanent! Just moved in this week, more like squatters, really.'

The Inspector frowned at him and Doctor Simmonds fell resentfully silent.

'With whom exactly do you reside?' he asked.

Alice told them Michael's name, his former address and his occupation. The Inspector asked his age and looked at her from under his eyebrows when she told him that Michael was twenty.

'Oh yes,' he said, as if the news were somehow very agreeable. 'And what is his home address?'

'He lives here,' Alice said foolishly. She could feel her cheeks were growing hot.

'I mean during the vacations,' the Inspector said stolidly. 'He's only a young lad, isn't he? He'd go home to his mum in the holidays.'

Alice swallowed. 'I don't know the precise address of his family,' she said. She gripped the pen to remind her that it was her behind the desk, it was her with a clean sheet of paper before her. She had committed no crime against persons (unless you counted Thomas the cat, and surely no one would send a CID officer around for a cat whose Life Force was already weak?). 'They live somewhere in Tunbridge Wells,' she said, clearing her throat.

The CID officer turned back the pages of his notebook to another marked place. 'Would that be

Mr and Mrs P. Coulter of 23 The Walk, Tunbridge Wells?' he asked.

Alice looked at the notebook as a little bird might look into the hypnotic eyes of a dancing snake. 'I don't know,' she said. 'It could be. You would have to ask Michael when he comes home.'

'Out, is he?' asked the Inspector, as if that were more than usually evasive.

'Yes,' Alice said. 'At the university,' she said. 'He went in for a lecture.' She heard a humble note in her voice, seeking praise for getting Michael off to work, as if the CID man was a truancy officer sent around by the university to fetch Michael into class.

'Did he drive in, Mrs Hartley? Do you have a car?'

'No,' Alice said. 'He had a lift in with some friends.'

'Do you *not* have a car?' the Inspector asked. 'A car, Mrs Hartley?'

Alice flushed slightly. 'We have a Jaguar,' she said.

'Ah,' the Inspector said pleasantly. 'Would that be the Jaguar CHH 100?'

'Yes,' Alice said in a very small voice.

Doctor Simmonds moved restlessly in his chair which tipped sideways but unfortunately he saved himself. 'Ask about the old lady!' he prompted irritably.

'All In Good Time,' the Inspector said firmly. He turned a page of the book and licked the stub of his pencil. 'Jaguar CHH 100, the property of Charles Henry Hartley, your husband?' he asked.

'Yes,' Alice said shortly.

'And you have this car in your possession?' he confirmed with irritating slowness.

'Yes,' Alice said again.

Inspector Bromley waited for Alice to volunteer how the car, which was never allowed anywhere but Professor Hartley's locked garage or his labelled parking space at the university, should come to be in the old stables of Rithering Manor stained and spotted with the pollen of rural spring and smelling strongly of fish and old seawater.

Alice, sensibly, said nothing.

'And now the house,' the Inspector said, turning a page. 'Does anyone else live here, in this house?' he asked. He eyed Alice acutely. 'I mean live. I mean alive.'

Alice shrugged her broad shoulders. 'Yes,' she said, on safer ground. 'Michael's Aunty Sarah lives here.'

'She can't!' snapped Doctor Simmonds at once. 'She can't! It's medically impossible!'

Alice's eyes blazed for a moment but she said nothing.

'You mean she is alive,' the CID man said slowly. When Alice nodded he wrote the words carefully down.

'That's not possible,' Doctor Simmonds said again. 'She is dead. I have filed the death certificate, and the funeral is booked for tomorrow.'

The Inspector cleared his throat. 'Would it be possible for us to see this . . . lady?' he asked.

Alice shrugged. 'I'll ask her if she'll see you,' she said. She got up from her chair and went out of the dining-room door to stand at the bottom of the stairs.

'Sarah!' she called.

'This is macabre!' the doctor exclaimed. 'I tell you, she's dead. I signed the certificate myself after a full examination.'

'Sarah!' Alice cried.

The doctor and the Inspector had followed Alice out into the hall.

'She's dead!' the doctor said again. 'Of course she won't answer.'

'She's alive!' Alice snapped, rounding on him at last. 'I can't help it if you can't tell a live person from a dead one. It's nothing to do with me! I'm not one of your patients, thank God. But I can tell you, after one of my herbal remedies, some herbal tea and a chance to express herself, she was out of that bed and happier and fitter than she has been for years. She has been down for her meals, she has been teaching classes. The other night she danced in the garden in the moonlight. Herbalism has given her a new lease of life. I have made her well!'

Doctor Simmonds was about to explode. 'Poppycock and quackery!' he shouted enraged. 'Witchcraft and nonsense! Corpses raised and corn circles in my hayfield. Don't think I don't know who's to blame for all this! And then telling the journalists that it's *my* influence. Good God! That's trespass and libel you're guilty of today alone! – and it's not even lunch-time yet!'

'Hold on a minute, Doctor Simmonds,' the Inspector said steadily. 'One at a time. Now, Mrs Hartley – you say you healed the old lady?'

Alice nodded, her colour high.

'And do you have a licence to practise medicine, Missus?' the Inspector asked, turning over a fresh page and licking the stub of his pencil again.

'I am a herbalist, not a quack,' Alice said with dignity. 'I do not need a licence. I have done evening classes. And at least I can tell whether a patient is alive or dead.'

Doctor Simmonds was a dangerous purple. 'You are half-way to being a witch, madam!' he said. 'You'd better mind your p's and q's! I can't tell you the amount of trouble you're in! There's practising medicine without a licence. There's fraud. There's trafficking in forbidden substances! There's running a bawdy house! There is offending against the planning regulations by change of use without prior planning consent, and there is kidnap!'

'Kidnap!' exclaimed Alice, stung. 'Michael is twenty! He chooses to live with me!'

'Not Michael,' the Inspector said slowly. 'The old lady, if the old lady is alive. Where is she now, Mrs Hartley?'

'She is resting,' Alice said defiantly. 'I'll go up and wake her. But I think you are being very unreasonable.'

She turned and went quietly up the stairs. Her heart was pounding at the list which Doctor Simmonds had reeled off. Half or more was nonsense.

But even half of it sounded serious. Alice had never spoken to a policeman before except to be considerately and gently moved on during a bottle-bank demonstration, and she did not like the way the CID officer was looking at her.

At the spare bedroom door she paused. The two of them had come up with her uninvited, and were at her shoulder.

'I think you are very selfish to upset an old lady's rest,' Alice said with dignity.

She raised her hand and knocked on the door.

'Sarah,' she said softly. 'It's me, Alice. Can I come in please?'

There was no reply.

Alice knocked again, a little louder.

Gently she turned the handle of the door. The door swung open.

The bed had been dragged over to the window so that the leg of the bed formed a handy anchor for the rope of knotted sheets which had been tied to it and flung out of the window.

Alice, Doctor Simmonds and the CID officer raced across the room to peer out of the window.

The rope of sheets reached to the ground; there was no sign of anyone outside.

'Aunty Sarah!' Alice yelled in sudden panic from the window out to the empty garden.

The wind blew through the newly pruned apple trees. The scent of the stocks and lavender wafted into the room from the newly weeded beds.

'Aunty Sarah!' Alice cried again, despairingly.

The CID officer leaned over and gently swung the window shut.

'Now then,' he said. 'Just you come downstairs, Hartley, while I phone for the lads and the dogs and we get to the bottom of this.'

Alice preceded them downstairs, her red gown billowing behind her, and back into the dining-room with her head held high and her heart pounding. She looked magnificent. She felt wretched.

'Officer, you are making a mistake,' she said.

'All in good time,' he replied evenly. 'May I use your telephone?'

Alice waved him towards the hall. Through the open door she could hear him conferring with headquarters and requesting assistance on the case. She repressed a shiver of dread.

Doctor Simmonds prowled around the dining-room, his glance avid, his aura electric with excitement. 'I think you are going to find yourself in a lot of trouble, Mrs Whatever-your-name-is!' he said smugly under his breath. 'A lot of trouble.'

Alice looked at him with disdain. 'And I think *you* are going to stay the same for the rest of your life,' she said firmly. 'I know which of us I'd rather be.'

The doctor took some time to understand that curse – the worst Alice could imagine. By the time it sank in, the CID officer was back in the doorway.

'I've asked for assistance,' he said magisterially. 'It seems to me that there is a case to answer.'

Alice went back to her seat behind the table. Her hands were trembling. She put them in her lap so the policeman could not see them.

'About what?' she asked. Her voice was firm, without a tremor.

'The disappearance of the old lady,' the Inspector said. 'If she is dead, as Doctor Simmonds here attests, then where is the body? If she is alive and happy as you claim, then where is she? And why has someone escaped from out of the window? You can understand that knotted sheets and an open window look a little suspicious in a house with adequate stairs, and a front door as well as a rear or tradespersons' entrance.'

Alice threw her head back and laughed in relief. 'That is nonsensical, officer!' she exclaimed. 'Whatever else you may believe about me, I simply would never kidnap anyone, or keep them against their will. My whole life, my whole philosophy, is that people should be free.'

Just at that moment there was the throaty roar of a motorbike and a small avalanche of shingle as a large Harley Davidson zoomed up the drive and stopped in a shower of stones. Jon-Jo, the husband of Louise and father (though he did not yet know it) of Daniel, kicked down the stand, heaved his bike on to it, removed his helmet and strode purposefully up the steps. Doctor Simmonds, speeding on his own adrenalin, scurried to the door and flung it open. Jon-Jo marched in.

'I've come for my wife,' he said in a stentorian

shout which would be invaluable should the revolutionary army need a sergeant-major. His fiery gaze
swept the room and lighted on Alice. 'You,' he said
with loathing. 'Bourgeois false-conscious jackal.
You have kidnapped my wife! She didn't come
home last night and she left me a note to say that
your disciples – poor blind brain-washed idiots –
were bringing her here. I've come for her and I
want her back. And I want an explanation.'

Doctor Simmonds's face was a picture of delighted malice. The policeman looked frankly over-
whelmed. '*Another* kidnap?' he asked, opening his
notebook and looking doubtfully at Alice. His tone
seemed to imply that one kidnap was criminal; two
was just greedy.

'Nonsense,' Alice said briskly. 'Louise came here
last night in a fatigued and depleted state thanks to
your appalling treatment of her. She has given birth
to a healthy baby boy, and the two of them will be
staying with me.'

Jon-Jo staggered backwards. 'A boy?' he asked.

'Which hospital did you take her to?' Doctor
Simmonds asked nastily. 'And which practitioner
cared for her during her confinement? *I* was not
called.' He nodded at the policeman as if to remind
him to take notes.

'She did not need a hospital,' Alice said fiercely.
'She was not ill. She did not need a doctor – least of
all one who cannot tell if a patient is alive or dead!
She needed love and support. She needed to be in
touch with the elements. She gave birth assisted by

her new friends – people and dolphins. It was a beautiful and moving moment, and she and the baby are perfectly well.'

'Dolphins?' Jon-Jo asked blankly. 'Dolphins?'

The Inspector flipped his notebook backwards to another marked page. He was sweating now, his fingers stuck to the paper of his notebook as he turned from one page to another. His fingers trembled, his heart sang. At this rate his department would have the highest clear-up rate of crimes in the whole country, possibly in the whole history of crime-fighting. The Home Secretary would mention them in speeches. Neighbourhood Watch committees would call them in! All of the crimes which had occurred in Brighton in the last four days could be blamed on Alice in one enormous and time-saving trial.

'Would this have anything to do with the theft of four dolphins named Peety, Tutu, Bibby and Bilbo from Sargent's Oceanside Marine Park last night? The watchman claimed that he saw a grey Jaguar driven by a naked woman.' He nodded thoughtfully. 'We did not believe him at the time,' he said frankly. 'But now, Mrs Hartley, you are making me wonder. Was that your Jaguar car? Were you the naked woman? And where are the dolphins?'

'Bugger the dolphins!' the doctor burst in, enraged. 'Where is Miss Coulter?'

'Where is my wife?' Jon-Jo yelled.

Alice had felt tired when she awoke that morning. And now all this stress and negative energy was draining her resistance. She put her head on her arms on the table and burst into tears.

'I think I had better telephone for more assistance,' the CID man said again.

Doctor Simmonds snorted. 'You'd do better to arrest her and take her down to the station,' he said. 'I'd have thought you'd have had enough against her by now! Two charges of kidnap, practising medicine without a licence, practising midwifery without a licence, stealing dolphins! Trespass on my hay meadow. Libel! What more d'you want?'

The CID man shook his head. 'We'll do this my way, if you don't mind, Sir,' he said reprovingly and left the room with his heavy tread.

'Where's my wife?' Jon-Jo asked insistently.

Alice lifted her tear-stained face. 'Do you love her?' she asked curiously.

Jon-Jo shuffled and looked at his feet. 'The revolution does not recognize the bourgeois mystification around the so-called emotions which operate merely to entrap the cadres, and to demoralize and mislead the workers,' he said fiercely.

'Then why do you want her back?' Alice asked simply.

Jon-Jo looked straight into Alice's eyes. 'Her father's going to do me over if I can't tell him where she is and show him his grandchild.'

'He sounds like a good man,' Alice said.

'So where is she?' Jon-Jo demanded.

The CID man reappeared in the doorway and awaited Alice's answer.

'She's upstairs, resting,' Alice said.

Doctor Simmonds gave one disbelieving snort. 'Again!' he said nastily. 'Another one of your patients upstairs resting. No doubt she will have flown up the chimney by the time we get there!'

'Can we see her?' the CID man interrupted.

'Of course,' Alice replied.

Once more she led the way upstairs. Once more she paused at a bedroom door, tapped on it, asked if she might come in, and pushed the door open.

The CID man mentally braced himself for another empty room and curtains blowing from an open window.

Louise was sitting up in bed, her white nightgown open at her large blue-veined milk-filled breasts. Her dark hair fell in soft ringlets around her face and tumbled over her shoulders. Her face was downturned, to watch her baby while he fed. There was a little half-smile on her lips.

Daniel the dolphins' godson was sucking contentedly, his blue eyes half closed in contentment, his rosebud mouth a perfect 'oo' of delight. One clenched fist beat gently at the air, the fine brown hair on his head stirred with his mother's breath. The tiny concave hollow at the centre of his head pulsed gently with his steady heartbeat. As they watched, Louise touched the tender crown of his head with her hand, like a blessing.

She looked up as the door opened and saw Alice and Doctor Simmonds and Inspector Bromley, and her husband, but she wasted no more than a glance on them all.

'Yes?' she asked, her voice soft; she hardly took her eyes from her baby.

The CID man was temporarily lost for words. Louise was as simple and as lovely as an angel in a painting, her unwavering gaze fixed lovingly on her little son's face, the tenderness of her smile, her baby's milk-drenched contentment.

'I shall need to ask you some questions, Missus,' the CID man said, his voice hushed, almost awed. 'Could you come downstairs when you have finished with your baby?'

Louise raised her eyes and smiled at him, a Madonna-like smile of perfect radiance.

'Fuck off, pig,' she said.

There was a wailing noise of sirens from the lane which grew steadily louder and louder. Alice imagined the curtains twitching all the way down the lane and Patricia Simmonds's bright face behind the lace, like a demented over-dressed bride.

Three police cars drew up outside the house, followed by a white police van which bounced with excitement as the two Alsatian dogs inside coupled frantically.

'They'll have brought a warrant to search the house and grounds,' said Inspector Bromley. 'I take it you have no objection, Mrs Hartley?'

Alice shook her head. There was nothing she could say.

Jon-Jo glanced at Louise and encountered a look of such scorching disdain that he suddenly remembered that there was no tax on his motorcycle and that he would prefer to move it out of the way of the police cars. He led the way downstairs. Alice, Inspector Bromley and Doctor Simmonds followed.

The hall was very full of uniformed policemen and one small shabby man in overalls.

'That's her!' he said, as soon as he saw Alice. 'That's her. I saw her clearly, she smiled at me as she drove past. Stark naked she was!' His piggy eyes roved over Alice reminiscently. 'Stark naked,' he said again. 'Absolutely starkers. In her birthday suit, you might say. A fine figure of a woman if you like them substantial.'

'Is this a positive identification then?' the young constable asked. He flicked open his notebook and licked a stub of pencil.

The CID man nodded. 'You're sure?' he asked the watchman.

The man hesitated. 'It would help if I could see her with no clothes on again,' he volunteered.

'No,' Inspector Bromley said bluntly. 'Is this the woman? Yes or No?'

'Or don't know?' Alice suggested quickly.

The watchman leered at her. 'I know all right,' he said. 'Yes, it was her. In a great grey Jaguar.'

'My Jaguar to be precise,' said a voice and Charles Hartley walked into the hall through the open door, a picture of elegance in a new pale grey suit, a replacement for the clothes which had disappeared with Alice when she stole the wardrobes. 'Officer, I can identify the car in the garage as my car which my wife stole from its parking place in the university, and assaulted me at the same time.'

Alice stared at him. 'Charles, you traitor,' she said.

He looked at her for the first time. '*Is* it fancy dress?' he asked nastily. 'I had no idea!'

Alice looked from him to the watchman's beady eyes. The red gown, diaphanous and sweeping, had been just right this morning when she had been Alice Hartley of the Growth Centre, a woman of mystery and power. Now she felt chilled and half undressed, and she wanted something warmer.

'I should like to change my clothes,' she said to Inspector Bromley, ignoring the rest of them.

'All right,' he said. He nodded to one of the policemen who fell into step behind Alice as she went upstairs. 'Constable Jones here will wait outside your bedroom door and bring you back down again.' He paused. 'And there are police officers in the garden,' he said stiffly. 'We'll have no more knotted sheets out of the window today.'

Alice nodded.

'In the meantime we'll take a little look around,' he said. He moved towards the dining-room and opened the door.

'My table!' Charles exclaimed. 'My rosewood Queen Anne dining-table and matching chairs!'

'I think we'd better have a note of all of this,' Inspector Bromley said wearily. The young policeman nodded and licked his pencil again. As Alice went slowly up the stairs she could hear from down below Charles's constant falsetto squeak of shock and anger. 'My Habitat Sofa! My Special Executive Rocker-Recliner Chair! My Leather Chesterfield Suite! My Wilton Carpet! My Television! My Bang and Olufsen Hi-Fi System! My Freezer! My Percolator! My Microwave!' And then, more horrified, 'She's scratched my Le Creuset Non-Stick Pans. She's dented them! Look at that!'

MONDAY AFTERNOON

Michael and his parents stood on the doorstep of Aunty Sarah's house. The drive was crowded with police cars and a police van, but the front door, usually hospitably open, was now tight shut. The place was oddly silent and from the windows idle policemen watched the Coulter family incuriously.

'Don't you have a key?' his father said impatiently.

Michael turned around, his young face defeated. 'It never used to be locked,' he said.

'There, there,' his mother said. Michael's mother was full of useful sayings like: 'Never mind then,' and 'It'll all come out in the wash.' And, 'It's a long road which has no turning.'

'Least said, soonest mended,' she said.

They could hear footsteps approaching down the hall. The door swung open.

Michael jumped. It was not Alice opening the door, it was not even Aunty Sarah. It was a large uniformed policeman. Behind him was a man in a suit, which Michael thought rather well cut. (It should be remembered that Michael was very young.)

'Bring 'em in,' the man said. 'You're Michael Coulter, aren't you?'

'Yes, Sir,' Michael said. He offered no explanation to his parents as to why he should be admitted to his Aunt's house by a uniformed policeman and a CID officer. This was because he had none. As they went into the house an Alsatian dog especially trained to sniff for drugs leered malevolently at Michael's ankles, making him jump.

'What is this all about, officer?' Michael's father demanded.

Inspector Bromley nodded at the uniformed police officer who drew Michael's parents into the parlour on their right while he took Michael into the sitting-room on their left. Michael dully watched the door shutting on his parents. He had a prescient awareness that the best moments of his life were probably over. He wondered sadly what his mother and father had done, and what greed or what folly had tempted them to crime so serious that they were being arrested today in Sussex. He sighed.

'I'll do everything I can to help you, officer,' he said nobly. 'You'll understand that I am very shocked. I really had no idea.' He paused for a moment's thought. 'I can't really believe my mother would have been mixed up in it,' he said. 'Whatever they have done, it would mainly be my father.'

Inspector Bromley did not waste a lot of time on Michael. It took three seconds to explain to him that it was not his parents who were in trouble, and something like ten minutes to reduce him to a weeping fourth-former. A further ten minutes later and Michael had signed a full and complete statement of all the events ever since he had first aided Mrs Hartley in her burglary of the marital home.

'I didn't realize I was doing anything wrong,' he said feebly.

'Of course you didn't, son,' the CID officer said gently. 'But there have been a lot of things going on here which are outside the law and we don't want a young lad like you mixed up in them.'

Michael had a brief fleeting vision of the days when he was not 'a young lad like you', but a master of sexual arts for whom middle-aged women changed their hairdressing appointments, lied to their husbands, and paid thirty pounds a visit. Of the brief time when he had been everything in the world to the witch-goddess Mrs Hartley. Of the young god he had been when Mrs Hartley bundled her husband in blue nylon car wrap so that she could drive him wherever he wanted to go in a custom-built concourse-condition Jaguar.

Michael sighed.

He had never thought it would last. But he had not thought it would end so suddenly and in the hands of the law.

'Any idea where she buried the old lady, son?'

Michael guppled. 'The old lady? Aunty Sarah?'

The policeman nodded.

'Aunty Sarah's not dead!' he exclaimed. 'She was

perfectly well when I saw her last night. She was more active every day. Why! She baby-sat for us last night, when we went out to help Louise give birth with the dolphins.' Michael paused. 'Well, she was a bit pissed,' he volunteered honestly.

The policeman consulted his notes. 'Was that the supper in which the toadstools known as "magic mushrooms" were consumed with the result of food-poisoning and 'allucinations for the vicar?' he asked.

'No!' Michael exclaimed. 'That was earlier! And anyway, the vicar wasn't hallucinating. He really did see Aunty Sarah. He was just upset because Alice doesn't like Series Two communion.'

The police constable who was taking notes in the corner breathed heavily as he puzzled over whether communion had one or two m's followed by one or two n's.

Inspector Bromley paused. 'His wife has testified that he was 'allucinating all the way home,' he said. 'She called in at Doctor Simmonds's, and he examined the aforesaid vicar and has made a statement to us to the effect that the man was drugged up to the eyeballs. Apparently he spoke in an abrupt and abusive manner to Doctor and Mrs Simmonds, he took his wife home and behaved quite unlike himself for the rest of the evening.'

Michael's jaw dropped as he thought of Maurice weeping into the sofa while Alice turned him over with her toe, and then Maurice going home with his energy released to storm and rage.

'Was he violent with his wife?' he asked, appalled.

The CID man consulted his notes. 'She said: "He Was Like A Madman,"' he read slowly. 'She said: "It Was Absolutely Terrific."'

The policeman in the corner blinked, a puzzled frown on his face.

'Anyway,' Inspector Bromley said, recovering ground rapidly. 'That's the doctor's testimony – that the vicar was hallucinating. And we have it on record that he thought he saw your Aunty Sarah at the supper table.'

'She was with us for supper,' Michael said desperately. 'She gets up for her meals now all the time.'

The CID man rose a little on his toes and subsided again looking severely at Michael. 'Now, now,' he said. 'We know that Miss Coulter is dead because Doctor Simmonds signed her death certificate.'

'She seemed dead,' Michael said helpfully. 'But then she had some of Alice's herbal tea and she came round.'

'Mrs Hartley cured her?' the CID man asked. 'Of death?'

Michael blushed unstoppably at the thought of Alice trying to poison Aunty Sarah. 'Not exactly,' he said weakly. 'But none of us knew how nice she was then. Alice gave her the herbal tea to, kind of, help her off.'

'Mrs Hartley poisoned her?' the CID man demanded. 'Is this before or after the signing of the death certificate?'

'After,' Michael said helpfully. 'But only a little bit after. Just after Doctor Simmonds left, actually. Then we thought she was dead and we went out, and then when we came back she got better and better, and now she is quite well.'

The constable in the corner was so fascinated by this story that he had forgotten to take notes. He met the CID man's eyes and they exchanged a quick shrug. Michael, it was clear to both of them, was permanently out to lunch. Criminal proceedings would be largely a waste of time. The young man was off his trolley.

'If your Aunty Sarah is quite well,' the CID man said, speaking slowly and clearly as if he was demonstrating how to make a tank out of a cotton reel and two matchsticks for the under-fives on Play School. 'If your Aunty Sarah is quite well, making soup for vicars, drinking herbal tea and baby-sitting, then where is she now?'

Michael fell silent.

He looked around the room.

'Well, I don't exactly know,' he said eventually. 'You see, I've been out all morning, and I've only just come in, she could be anywhere really.'

The CID man nodded. 'That'll be all for now,' he said. 'We'll go next door and join your parents and the others.'

Michael nodded miserably. There was the sound of car wheels on the drive. The room flashed with the blue rotating light of a police car.

'What's that?' Michael asked peevishly.

The Inspector looked out of the window as the car lined up to park with others on the drive. 'Drug squad's already here,' he said. 'So it could be the vice squad about the brothel charge, or the fraud squad about the fraud charges, or the lads from the Serious Incident Unit about the two kidnaps and the murder,' he said. 'No,' he corrected himself. 'It's the local bobby, come about the trespass and criminal damage to the hayfield. He went off to fetch the trespass forms after he brought the husband.'

'Husband?' Michael said, totally at sea. 'I didn't know Aunty Sarah had a husband?'

'Not Aunty Sarah,' the CID officer explained with elaborate scorn. 'Mrs Hartley. You remember, Professor Hartley, at your university. Him that's going to invigilate at your exams at the end of this term. Him that gets to decide whether you pass or fail after three years' work and no chance of a re-take. The bloke whose wife you nicked, whose house you stripped, whose car you stole.'

'Oh, *that* husband,' Michael said.

'Come on,' the CID man said. 'Let's make a family party of it. I want to know what's going on.'

Michael blinked at him owlishly. He did not share this chummy curiosity. He had no feelings except a profound need for a good meal and a long rest. He had a sense, forgivable in one who, though very much more experienced than the average twenty-year-old, was nonetheless still quite young, that it was all a bit too much for him and he should not be asked to deal with it.

'Come on,' the constable said, not unkindly. 'Face the music. You'll be getting off lightly. The husband won't kill you. He's been quite calm about it all, really.'

Useless for Michael to remember that it was Charles Hartley's calm which was responsible for the whole sorry business. He was propelled from the room by the unfeeling Inspector, and then taken over in the hall by his bracing father who swooshed him into the lounge into the middle of a conversation between Alice Hartley and her estranged husband, Charles.

Alice was quite unlike herself.

Michael had seen her in half a dozen bright coloured dresses with trailing skirts and fringed shawls. He had never thought she had ordinary clothes at all. But there she was, sitting on one of Professor Hartley's hessian-covered chesterfield chairs by the cold fireplace, dressed in a pair of jeans and a dark coloured sweatshirt, her face shiny from soap and water, her eyes pink and swollen from crying, her hair drawn back from her face in a greasy ponytail, her colour pale. She looked like a woman who has been arrested in Fine Fare for lifting half a pound of cheese. She looked like a woman who phones in to mid-morning consumer programmes to complain of psychosomatic gynaecological ailments. She looked like a woman who gets migraine, and back pains, and premenstrual tension. She looked like a woman who gets allergies, and nervous eczema. She looked like a woman who has lost.

'Oh, Alice,' Michael said, and his young voice was full of pity.

Charles and Alice looked around. Charles frowned and then recognized him. 'Oh, it's you,' he said redundantly.

Michael nodded, as if grateful for the confirmation. 'Yes,' he said.

Alice said nothing at all.

'I see you've met my mother and father,' Michael said politely. 'I told you they would pop down to see us.'

She nodded, her dark eyes dulled. 'Michael, where is Aunty Sarah?' she demanded. 'Do you know? They all think we killed her, Michael! Where is she? When I went into her bedroom, it looked like she climbed out of the window. Why would she do that? Where can she be?'

Michael shrugged helplessly. 'I told them that you changed your mind about poisoning her when she had such a strong Life Force and survived after your first attempt,' he said helpfully.

Alice's eyes darkened with despair. 'Thanks very much,' she said bitterly.

Michael paused, then he glanced at Charles Hartley and cleared his throat. 'Alice,' he said tentatively. 'I don't want to seem stupid, but am I right in thinking that it is all over between us?'

There was a silence. The room had always seemed so airy and spacious; but now it was filled with many people. Professor Hartley, Michael's mother, Michael's father, Doctor Simmonds, a couple of uniformed policemen, Jon-Jo sitting as quietly as he could in the corner and trying to be invisible, the CID man, the drug squad man with one of the sniffer dogs, Michael – and Alice, who sat so still and so silent by the empty hearth.

'It's all over for me at any rate,' she said dully. 'Whether it's prison at home or prison at prison, it's all over for me.'

It was very quiet for a moment. Then from far away down the lane came the moaning wail of another police car and in a few moments it had turned up the drive.

'Fraud squad,' said Inspector Bromley. 'Brought their own warrant.'

As the front door opened and a man yelled as the other sniffer dog bit him, there was another wail from down the lane, abruptly cut off as the police car shut off the siren and turned down Aunty Sarah's narrow drive.

'Serious crimes squad,' the CID man said. 'About the murder and the kidnap, with their warrant. Forensic lads will be along in a moment. They'll have the lawn up in no time. First thing they will look at is those newly dug flower-beds. Best you make a full confession, Mrs Hartley. That's my advice. We think you hid the old lady's body and pretended you had cured her; or else she recovered after the doctor's visit and then you murdered her and buried her on the premises. I'd come clean if I was you, Mrs Hartley.'

A bright-faced old man in khaki shorts biked up

the drive and leaned his bicycle against the ornamental stone flowerpots at the front of the house. He straightened the toggle around his khaki shirt and whistled a bright little glee as he skipped blithely up the steps.

The drug squad dog growled nastily at him as he put his head around the door.

'Looking for the householder,' he said cheerily.

'Why is that then, Sir?' Inspector Bromley said cautiously.

'District Commissioner for Brighton Scouts, Hutchen's the name, the lads call me Rabbit – get it? Hutchen ... Hutch ... Rabbit Hutch ... Rabbit!'

'Yes, Mr Rabbit,' the Inspector said wearily. 'Why did you want the householder here?'

Hutchen looked around the room, missing his friend Doctor Simmonds in the crowd. 'There's been a complaint about abuse of Boy Scouts on these premises,' he said confidentially. 'Employing them in a bawdy house under the direction of chorus girls. Could be very nasty. It's the sort of thing I like to be very careful about.'

'Vice squad,' Inspector Bromley said promptly. 'Not my direct responsibility right now. You'll have to wait your turn, Sir, and these gentlemen will take you next door for a full statement.'

'Right you are!' Hutchen said briskly, throwing a salute at the vice squad men.

'Now then,' Inspector Bromley said gently to Alice. 'Seems that the longer we stay here the more charges come in. Hadn't you better make a clear simple statement so that we can all go home and get our dinners? Except for you, that is,' he said fairly.

Alice looked around fearfully at all the closed faces.

Michael's parents, his ghastly mother, so near her own age, with her silly amiable smile and her badly cut red silk suit, staring at Alice full of repressed Oedipal desire and open envy. His father, red-faced and champing, but none the less deeply excited at being in on a kill to rival any fox-hunt in Kent. The drug squad with their mean faces and remarkably dilated pupils, lounging in the doorway, the vice squad with their hands moving rhythmically in their pockets, lost in a world of their own.

As she looked around she heard the back door open and heard the vicar's nervous voice say from the hall: 'I thought there might be a place for a totally neutral voice here, saying . . . "now just wait a moment, I believe we can look at this in a positive way".'

'Oh God,' Alice said in misery.

In the hall the dog growled sulkily at the vicar's sandals and jeans and Greenpeace t-shirt. 'Hello!' Maurice said irrepressibly, as he came into the room. He looked around and saw the tableau around Alice, like outraged peasants heaping faggots around the bare vulnerable feet of a long-ago witch.

'Quite a party,' he said cheerily. 'But I wonder if there's a place here for someone who – while not an expert by any means – has maybe thought about these issues a little? Maybe someone like me who can say, "Now come on let's all sit down together and think this thing through"? Someone who can bring a bit of common sense, and a drop of training, and a little idea of how things ought to be and say: "Come *on*, gang, let's work with the flow rather than against it!"'

The CID man shot a look at the drug squad man. 'Is he high now?' he asked under his breath. 'He sounds like it.'

The drug squad dog whined. The drug squad man tapped the vicar gently on the shoulder. 'Would you just come in here, Sir?' he said politely. 'I'd like to check a few things with you.'

Maurice beamed, delighted. In all the years since his ordination no one had ever voluntarily asked him to spend some time with them.

'Oh, of course!' he said. 'Of course! All the time in the world. You just tell me what's on your mind and I'll see if I can help you with it.'

They went into the library together and Alice caught a glimpse of the two wives behind him: the vicar's wife, and the doctor's wife, who had been so quick to spot wrong-doing and so foolish not to grasp the opportunity to do a little wrong themselves.

Alice sighed. She hadn't liked them personally but that would never have stood in their way. All they would have had to do was ask, pay an astronomical enrolment fee, and they too could have done whatever they liked with whoever was available.

It all seemed such an utter waste! Such a miserable ending to what had been such a wonderful idea! Such a death of life! Of libido! Of freedom! Probably a death of Jungian archaic myths too for all Alice knew!

'Shit,' she said under her breath.

Professor Hartley looked down at her and frowned. It was his 'I know better than you' frown. Alice had seen it before. Oh! For years and years and years.

'Keep your voice down, dear,' he said levelly. 'I should have thought that even you would see that you are in enough trouble as it is.'

'Professor Hartley.' Inspector Bromley stepped forward. A lump over his heart was making strange gargling noises. Alice assumed it was a pacemaker of some sort and looked at his face to see signs of heart strain. She was rather surprised when his pacemaker said brightly: 'Roger!' and then fell silent.

'Professor Hartley,' the officer said. 'Will you be accompanying your wife to the county police headquarters? We will have to charge her formally.'

'Of course, officer!' Charles said blithely. You would have thought he was enjoying this. And, gentle reader, you would have been spot on. 'Certainly! I take it there could be no objection to me driving down in my own car? There is no dispute that the accused stole my car shortly after looting my house?'

The CID man cocked an eyebrow at Alice.

Dumbly, she shook her head.

No, there was no denying it. The world had fallen about her ears, and she was going to carry the can. The only worry left to her, like the last surviving twitch in a landed, dying fish, was where was Aunty Sarah? And whoever would care for her when Alice was serving life imprisonment, and Michael and his red-faced father had forgotten all about her again? Alice could see her own future clearly. The long consecutive prison sentences, the greyness of day after day in Holloway – or worse, somewhere bright and cheerful where they would make her take OU degrees and mad peers of the realm would mount campaigns for her early release.

But that was not the worst prospect. When she was banished from the normal world Sarah would be alone again. Alone and with nothing to do except to stay in bed and torment Daisy, the daily help.

'I shan't invite my wife to drive with me,' Charles said smoothly. 'Under the circumstances,' he smiled with veiled triumph at the policeman, 'under the circumstances I can't think it would be entirely appropriate. Anyway, I take it she will have to go with you in the police car?'

'I'm afraid so, Sir,' the policeman answered.

'Handcuffed?' Charles asked hopefully.

'I don't think that will be necessary,' Inspector Bromley said.

Alice knew that Charles was disappointed. He would have preferred her to have been carried out of the house with a ball and chain on each wrist and ankle and flung on a tumbril amid a jeering mob of sansculottes and dragged off to the guillotine without delay.

'We'll also charge the young man,' the Inspector said heavily, gesturing to Michael.

'As an accessory, merely, I assume,' Michael's father said fiercely.

Inspector Bromley nodded judicially. 'It depends, Sir, on whether he is prepared to give evidence against his former partner, Hartley. He has been very helpful with our inquiries. He will only be charged as an accessory for the more serious offences of fraud, kidnap and murder.'

'He'll help. Won't you, darling?' his mother said, resting her hand on Michael's sleeve. 'After all, a stitch in time saves nine.'

'Yes, Sir,' he said miserably.

He met Alice's dark tear-filled gaze for only one moment and then his pale glance fell to the ground.

'I'd like to say I'm very sorry, Sir,' he said. 'I see now that it has all been a mistake.'

(The weedy Judas.)

'Fine,' Inspector Bromley said brightly, and turned to Professor Hartley. 'After you, Sir,' he said.

They went out through the door together, almost arm in arm, and paused on the steps surveying the mayhem which had once been the wooded front garden. Sniffer dogs were scurrying around digging frantically at the site of old forgotten bones. Policemen were resting on their shovels, digging long scientific slit trenches through the undergrowth and over and around strong tree roots. The newly weeded herbaceous border was uprooted and dying on the drive. The newly mown lawn was trodden and muddy with the track of boots.

Alice paused in the doorway with a policeman from the drug squad at her right hand and one from the vice squad at her left. She heard Inspector Bromley ask her estranged husband if he personally would go to the witness box to testify that she was clinically insane.

'It'd be probably best to get one of your friends to do it for you,' the policeman advised. 'Not very nice to stand up in the box and tell a jury that your wife is barking. It'd put a bit of a strain on your marriage when she does get out.'

'If she ever gets out,' Charles replied cheerfully. 'I would have thought that the best thing for her would be to have her detained until she can demonstrate that she is completely cured.'

'Can take some time that,' Inspector Bromley said cautiously.

Charles smiled. 'Oh,' he said, 'with a bit of ECT and some heavy medication, some aversion therapy, and dogmatic Freudian analysis, she should be fit to rejoin society in something between ten and twenty years. It's the sort of thing I have an interest in. I might undertake her case myself, actually. She won't be the same woman of course. That sort of treatment knocks the life out of them I always find. But it's the best thing for society. And it'll be the best thing for her in the long run.

'She'll thank me in the end,' he said cheerfully. 'I've tried to live with her hysteria for years, you know. She's been in counselling for most of our marriage. God knows, no man has ever tried harder to manage a woman who was simply *beyond* control.'

The Inspector nodded. He found he was warming to Charles. While he had no specific complaint to issue against Mrs Bromley (who led a blameless if deathly existence in Ditchling), he rather liked the grand forensic manner in which Charles anatomized his wife's failings.

'One expects women to be unreasonable,' Charles said largely. 'It is their chemical and biological make-up. They are not creators – there are no women artists, composers, sculptors. They lack logical thought processes – there are no women mathematicians or philosophers. What really are they good for?'

Inspector Bromley shrugged. Faced with the direct question he was damned if it were not unanswerable. What, after all, was Mrs Bromley good for? She ran the house, shopped and prepared all his food, cared for his two children, and supported and serviced his needs. But what did she *do* all day?

'I'll tell you what they are good for!' Charles proclaimed. 'They are the support team to the thinkers. They are the second-in-commands. They are the back-stop. Their job is to organize one's life in such a way that a man can give his best to society. A man like me, for instance, whose life is so full of challenges and creative struggle that his home life must be . . .' Charles paused for effect, 'flaw-less,' he pronounced.

Inspector Bromley nodded. His life, too, de-manded a flawless home. 'But women won't do it,' he mourned.

Charles smiled smugly. Miranda Bloomfeather was taking her finals this year and knew of only one way to scrape an honours pass. Miranda Bloom-feather would give Charles a flawless home. Miranda Bloomfeather would have done anything on God's earth to please Charles. (But only until after finals.)

'Some will,' Charles said. 'Properly adjusted ones will.'

Alice felt rage slowly building inside her, heating up like a bonfire, but it scorched only herself. She knew there was nothing she could do. One large policeman stood one side of her, another stood the other. They were not actually holding her, but they were looming, confident in the size of their boots and the blueness of their uniforms. Alice dawdled unwillingly between the two of them, helpless, help-less, hopeless just like all of her married life.

Charles and Inspector Bromley went out through the front door and preceded Alice down the steps and across the drive to the waiting police car. Only one half of the double front door was open, the policemen fell back to let Alice go first.

Half-way across the drive her husband and Inspec-tor Bromley had paused to discuss bail and how

Professor Hartley could legitimately avoid ever having his wife home again. Alice, in a scene reminiscent of Paul Scofield going to the scaffold as Sir Thomas More, looked up at the poignantly blue sky, breathed her last gasp of freedom and prepared herself to abandon hope.

There was an almighty squeal of tyres and a shriek of brakes as Professor Hartley's concourse-condition silvery-grey Jaguar whirled like an unleashed fiend around the corner from the stable block.

The car bore down upon the Professor as if it wanted revenge for all those hours and hours of boredom, blinded under the blue plastic sheet. Professor Hartley leaped vertically upward and windmilled his arms to get clear. It clipped him as it roared past, throwing him against Inspector Bromley and backwards into the rose bushes.

The policemen guarding Alice were stunned into immobility at the broad daylight vision of Inspector Bromley collapsing among the rose bushes in the arms of the husband of their prisoner.

But Alice was already running; running blindly, instinctively, without a thought in her head, only guided by the hunted animal's instinct for escape, running down the drive after the car.

It screamed to a standstill, the passenger door swung open, the motor roared.

'GET IN!' screeched Aunty Sarah, loud as a banshee, like a hag on a speeding broomstick. Her rats' tails hair streamed loose over her white pintucked nightie. Her purple toque hat with the nodding egret feathers was madly askew. A bottle of elderflower champagne fizzed and cascaded beside the gear lever. 'GET IN, my darling! Let's show 'em who's boss!'

And Alice Hartley: mad, bad Alice Hartley, her face once again alight with joy, leaped for the passenger door, slammed it on the policeman's scrabbling hand, and fell into the bucket seat as the powerful car sprayed gravel and roared, triumphantly, away.